ONE SMALL BITE

R. J. Hanrahan

ISBN:0692523766
ISBN-13: 978-0692523766

DEDICATION

To my wonderful wife Patricia, who has been my rock, my inspiration and occasionally my kick in the ass. My twin sons, Carrick and Callum, who are turning out to be not only smart and good looking like their dad, but they are perfect gentlemen, something one does not find in this day and age.

To my mother, who did everything in her power to make sure my brothers and I had the best of everything. To my dad, I wish I knew you better, but some day I pray we will meet again.

To my agent and mentor Vaughn Thompson I send all my love for putting up with me and my obsessive compulsive behavior and connecting me with Jean Marie Stanberry who turned out to be more than an editor and a critic, but a true inspiration to my entire writing process. She advised me to leave my heart on the page and that is exactly what I have done.

ACKNOWLEDGMENTS

The cover image is a composite of images created by artists at Kingsmuir Press using images by
xeodu4@freedigitalphoto.net
and AnusornPnachol@freedigitalphoto.net

This original piece of art may not be reproduced in any form and remains the property of Kingsmuir Press and author R. J. Hanrahan.

Visit us at kingsmuirpress.com

CHAPTER ONE

A loud crash and the sound of shattering glass raining into her room startled Pem awake from a sound sleep. She bolted upright in her bed, her confused brain trying to focus as her eyes darted anxiously around the room trying to make out exactly what had happened. It was difficult, it was the middle of the night and her room was shrouded in total darkness.

Pem let out a startled gasp of surprise as a flash of lightening illuminated the entire room for a split second. As this burst of brilliant light illuminated her room, she spotted a man, who was crouching there in her window.

The glass from the shattered window had rained down over her sleeping body, it littered her entire bed and glistened like the rain that was falling outside. The room was pitch black, lit only by the occasional flashes of lightening. Pem was slightly confused, but not frightened. She was staring numbly at this man who had just burst through her bedroom window. She didn't know him, but oddly enough, she didn't fear him. In fact, he seemed eerily familiar.

He was a young man, Pem guessed he was in his early twenties and he was classically handsome, with facial features like a Greek God that seemed to be chiseled from marble. He had flawless skin that was almost translucently white and his tousled hair was black and shiny. As far as she could tell, the man was dressed all in black, but he looked elegant, not like some criminal who had just broken into her house. This gentleman didn't look like any man she had ever seen before, but for some reason, his presence there in her bedroom didn't frighten her.

"Come with me Pem," said the man, extending his hand to her. Pem didn't hesitate for a moment, it seemed only natural to take it, there was nothing foreboding about this man.

Pem stepped gingerly through broken glass and   boldly took the hand of this complete stranger who had just burst into her room. Mindlessly going with this man went against everything she had ever been taught, but she couldn't seem to control her emotions or her actions. Though her mind was telling her this man was a stranger, her heart seemed to be telling her the opposite. This man was was strangely familiar, though she was certain they had never met.

The next thing she knew, she was flying through the air with her arms wrapped around his neck, her nightgown blowing around them as they flew rapidly through the night.

The dark clouds that hung over the valley seemed to be dispersing and the moon began to shine through, lighting their way.

It seemed only a matter of minutes before they arrived at his castle. It seemed to Pem that she had been immersed in a fairytale, her only fear was that she would wake up from this dream and it would be just that...a dream.

"Welcome home, Pem my Queen," said the man, bowing to her and kissing her hand gently.

Pem took a nervous step backwards. What did he mean, home? This was quite troubling, why would this man want her as his queen, she was a mere child, just eleven years old?

"What do you mean, your queen?" she asked, taking another careful step backwards. The delicious thrill of this adventure

seemed to be fading and she was suddenly feeling fearful of this strange situation.

"You are Pemberthy Parker, oldest daughter of Ludmilla, are you not?" asked the man, his eyes were a deep, luminous amber, they seemed to mesmerize her with their incessant fire.

"Yes," said Pem, trying to hide the sudden fear that seemed to be sneaking into her voice. What was she doing here, and why had she gone with the man so willingly?

"This my dear lady, is your destiny. On your eighteenth birthday you will return here to this castle to be married to me. On our marriage you will become Queen and we will rule this kingdom till our heirs come of legal age."

Pem shook her head numbly in an attempt to process what this man was saying. She was destined to be a queen? This did not even seem possible, there had to be some mistake. She was eleven years old. She lived in a tiny house in the suburbs, her family wasn't rich, in fact, they could barely be considered middle class. She was a B student, she had a bit of a stubborn streak and spent many weekends at home doing chores because she'd been grounded. These were clearly not makings of a Queen.

Pem suddenly felt herself surrounded by others. They all seemed to be watching her curiously as she attempted to process all of this. She looked around in wonder at the mass of people that were suddenly crowding around her. She felt as if she had been transported back in time, these people were all dressed like members of a medieval royal court. The woman were draped in gorgeous flowing silk dresses and the men wore heavy velvet tunics trimmed in gold.

They were all beautiful, with the same translucent ivory skin as the man who had brought her here. The women sank into deep curtsies, while the men bowed and nodded regally to her.

"Wait...who?" She didn't even know what she wanted to say. Who was this man, and who were all these people?

"Forgive me, I fear we have never been properly introduced, I am Fortuno of Urbino, your betrothed."

"My what?" gasped Pem. None of this was making any sense.

"You are my intended, my 'fiancee' as some would say. When you are eighteen we will marry and you will return to the castle and take your rightful place as the Queen of our Kingdom."

"No, I don't think so," said Pem, shaking her head in confusion. This was a dream, a very, very, weird dream.

"Do not despair, I know this sounds a bit overwhelming right now, but as I said, it is your destiny. You are of the Venezia bloodline, one of the most noble bloodlines in our coven. It is what the Urbino line needs to restore our coven to it's former glory," said Fortuno, smiling at her.

Pem was still staring at him numbly. She still wasn't sure who this man was, or what he wanted from her. Her mother's maiden name had been Venezia, but how could this man possibly know these things?

"I don't know who you are but you must take me home right now," cried Pem, her voice had a crescendo of panic in it. She couldn't believe she hadn't just screamed when this man came into her room.

"I have brought you here tonight for your own protection."

"No...wait, this must be a mistake," mumbled Pem, she was looking around for a way out, but she was completely surrounded by these strange looking people.

"Do not be afraid, these are your subjects, from this day on they have pledged their loyalty to you. They have sworn an ancient oath to protect their Queen. Once you receive the mark there is no force in the universe that shall be able to harm you," said Fortuno.

"No one wants to harm me!" snapped Pem, this man was frightening her, she just wanted to go home, this was crazy.

"Not now, but perhaps soon. You are so vulnerable in your human form, once you get the mark, your kingdom will protect you."

"Protect me from what? How can I possibly be a queen, I am only eleven years old," cried Pem. This all seemed completely ridiculous. She was a child, not a Queen.

"Age is but a number my fair Queen. You might be surprised to find out that I am over four hundred years old myself, though none of that will matter, once we are married.

Pem was standing there nervously trying to digest all this information. The only possible explanation was that this was all a dream, a crazy, crazy, dream.

Pem drew in an anxious breath as she realized the crowd of medieval worshippers was slowly closing in on her, one careful step at a time. What were they going to do to her? Pem's eyes darted around anxiously looking for a weak spot where she could break through the crowd, but there was none. Just before her ensuing panic could consume her, Fortuno reached out and took her by the arm.

"The wine," snapped Fortuno. His voice was hollow and businesslike all of a sudden. It made Pem's heart contort with fear.

A man approached them with a small carafe and a splendid gold goblet. The man poured the wine into the goblet and held it out in front of Pem.

"Drink the wine of thine kingdom," said the man holding it out in front of her.

"No!" snapped Pem shaking her head nervously.

"Please my lady, you must drink the wine," said Fortuno.

"No, I am not who you think. Ask my mother, this is a mistake."

Fortuno sighed miserably and placed his arms around her, restraining her. For some reason, the feel of his arms around her was strangely comforting. She wanted to struggle and fight off this man who was restraining her, but her body collapsed gently into his arms.

Pem could not fathom what was wrong with her, this was crazy. Fortuno gently held her as the man with the wine raised the cup to her lips. She pressed her lips closed as tightly as she could, but it was no use, some unknown force was making her drink the wine. Before she knew it, she had eagerly gulped down the entire goblet full.

She felt dizzy as Fortuno finally released her. He bowed to her and then to the crowd. The crowd erupted into cheers.

Pem wasn't sure why they were cheering, her head was spinning miserably as she struggled to glance around the room. She felt as if she were going to pass out, but she

didn't want to, it was so beautiful. Everyone was now kneeling before her on the floor chanting, chanting, chanting....

CHAPTER TWO

"Pem, Pem are you alright!"

Pem bolted straight up in bed as she heard her mother calling her name. Her mother was running frantically up the stairs. She was out of breath by the time she reached her side.

"Are you okay?" cried her mother, climbing into bed with her and hugging her.

"Yes," said Pem, looking around the room slightly bewildered.

The window above her bed was shattered and she was completely covered in glass. She had been in a castle, hadn't she? Had it merely been a dream? Now, she wasn't quite sure.

"Oh thank God, you have some cuts, but at least you're okay," breathed her mother, hugging her again.

"Where is he? There was a man," said Pem, still looking around her room in confusion, struggling to make herself wake up.

"What man?" cried her mother, her eyes darting nervously around the room.

"The man who burst through the window," said Pem.

"Pem darling, there was no man. It was a hail storm, it broke nearly every window in the house. Oh, I wish we hadn't put your bed there, right under the window," said her mother, stroking her hair gently.

"No, there was a man, I saw him. He could fly, he took me to his castle," said Pem, already starting to doubt herself.

"Oh Pem darling," her mother giggled, "it was just a dream. Your room is on the second floor, the hail broke the window and I guess you just dreamed the rest. You're going to be fine. Come on, I'll take you downstairs and get you cleaned up," said her mother, taking her by the hand and pulling her out of bed.

In a matter of minutes, Pem was in a hot bath and she was scrubbing herself with a washcloth. It was nice to be shut in the bathroom, away from all the commotion. She could hear her mother, her father and her grandpa in the living room, removing the old window panes from their frames so they could take them to the hardware store and get the glass replaced. Her baby sister Cora was whining annoyingly, the whole house was in an uproar.

The frosted glass window in their bathroom and Cora's bedroom window on the north side of the house were the only windows in the whole house that hadn't been broken by the hail storm.

Pem looked down at the cuts all over her body. Her bed sat right in front of her room's big window. Her room was on the second floor and it was long and narrow with a pitched roof, so it was really the only spot they could put her bed. She had woke up completely covered in glass. She had cuts on her face, her chest, her arms. None of the cuts really hurt too bad, except for two small marks on her neck. They were the smallest cuts of all, but for some reason they hurt the most. It made her entire neck feel sore.

It was weird how she had slept through the storm, she guessed she had just incorporated it into her dream. The breaking of her window had become the man crashing

through her window and the rest of the storm had turned into her flying away in the arms of some ancient evil creature.

It was Tuesday, but Pem and her sister didn't go to school. There was too much work to do, it turned out the school had closed for the day anyway. The storm had broken many of the windows at the school too.

After that day life went on as normal. Her cuts had healed except for the marks on her neck, they had healed into what looked like a birth mark, two tiny brown marks that resembled comas. Pem had completely forgotten about the man and her strange dream, till one day, more than a year later.

There was a massive snowstorm, nine inches of snow had fallen during the night and buried their neighborhood in a blanket of deep, white snow. School was called off, which was a good thing. Nobody was getting up the hill on their street till the snowplows went through.

Pem was happy, she loved snow. She bundled up in her warmest clothes so she could go sledding with her best friend Leah and her little sister Cora.

The road they lived on was a long hill, they lived three quarters of the way from the top, so they only had to drag their sleds part way up the hill, at least the first time, anyway.

Pem and Cora had a great sled, it was old, but in perfect condition, it had been their father's and they loved it.

When they reached the top of the hill Leah climbed on her sled and Pem and Cora climbed on theirs. Soon they were racing down the deep snow on the street. They screamed in delight as they sped past all the neighborhood dads out shoveling their driveways. When they reached the bottom of

the hill, they dragged their sleds up the hill behind them, so they could go down again.

The rest of the kids in the neighborhood were coming out too. They all wanted to get a few runs in before the snowplows came through. As they were trudging back up the hill Pem saw a face that distressed her. It was Eddy Grainger, the neighborhood bully.

Pem couldn't stand Eddy, in fact, she always did everything she possibly could, to avoid him, he was the meanest kid she had ever met.

Unfortunately, Eddy had already spotted her, he had stopped dragging his own sled up the hill and was now standing there at the end of her driveway, waiting for her. She couldn't even go home to avoid him.

"Hey Parker, nice sled," he called out to her, his voice was thick with sarcasm.

Pem had just arrived in front of him, rolling her eyes miserably. He was standing there at the foot of her driveway, looking her over carefully, a crooked smile on his lips.

"You lame asses wanna race?"

"Give me a break Eddy, do you really want to race a girl?" asked Pem, just wishing he would go away.

"Not really, but I'm bored already and I know I can beat you on that old piece of shit," he laughed.

"It's not a piece of shit," cried Pem, completely insulted.

"Sure it is, it's like a hundred years old. Just like your sister's coat," laughed Eddy.

Pem frowned in embarrassment, Cora's coat was old, it had been hers, and it had been her cousin Clarissa's before that. The sled was nearly an antique, it had been their dad's back in the 1950's, it was 1978, sure there were better sleds now, but their family didn't have much money.

Pem and Cora didn't have much, they were used to wearing hand me downs. No one had ever teased them about it before. Most of the kids in their neighborhood were in the same boat. You took what you could get and didn't complain, that's just how it was.

"Why don't you just go play with the boys," snapped Leah, she wasn't about to stand around and let Eddy Grainger insult her friends.

"Why don't you go home and cry to your mommy you ugly little cunt," he seethed, kicking her in the shin.

"Ow, you stupid punk!" cried Leah, lunging at him.

Eddy wrestled with her for a moment, Leah didn't have too much of a chance against him. He was older and bigger. Within moments he had wrenched his arm around her neck. Leah was gasping to breathe, he had a firm chokehold on her. Eddy was glaring down into her eyes and squeezing harder by the moment.

"Eddy, let her go, you're hurting her," cried Pem.

"That's the point, you little bitches are too cocky, you need to learn to respect your elders," seethed Eddy.

Leah's face was contorted in agony and she was literally gasping to breathe, Pem was panicking. What the hell was he trying to prove?

"Eddy please!" cried Pem, her voice raising in fear.

"I'll break this little bitch's neck, I swear I will. Do you believe me Pemberthy?" sneered Eddy, he was slowly tightening his grasp, choking her.

Pem was scared, Eddy was fifteen years old, the three of them didn't have a chance against him.

"Why do you have to be so mean all the time, just let her go," cried Pem, her whole body was shaking, she could run and tell her mom, but by that time Leah might be dead.

"What are you going to give me if I do?" he teased, flashing her a sardonic smile.

"You can have my sled," cried Pem, what else did she have to offer him? She truly had nothing.

Pem was panicking, Leah's gasping had stopped, her lips were turning blue and it was obvious she couldn't make a sound at all.

"I don't want that old piece of shit."snapped Eddy, wrenching his arm even tighter around Leah's neck.

"Just let her go Eddy."

"I will, if you give me what I want."

"What do you want Eddy?"

"I want you," said Eddy.

"What?" cried Pem.

"You heard me, if you come with me and do what I want, I'll let her go," said Eddy, his facial expression softening into an evil smile.

"What are you going to do?" asked Pem, her voice was shaky and weak. She was scared, Eddy was bad. Whatever he had planned for her was going to be bad.

"Whatever I want," said Eddy, flashing her a sly smile.

"No way!" cried Pem, he was disgusting, there was no way she was going anywhere with him.

"Fine, just stand there and watch while I snap your best friend's neck," seethed Eddy, wrenching his arm even tighter around Leah's neck. She was fading fast and couldn't even gasp for air now, her eyes had rolled back in their sockets and Pem almost feared she was already dead.

"Please just let her go, I'll do whatever you want," cried Pem, regretting her words the moment they left her mouth.

Eddy smiled and threw Leah roughly into the snow. Poor Leah could only lay there, gasping to catch her breath. Pem was completely horrified, she couldn't even move as she watched Leah struggling to sit up, the color was slowly returning to her cheeks.

"Come with me Pemberthy Parker, we're going to have some fun," said Eddy, motioning for her to follow him.

"Wait, at least let me take Leah home first," said Pem, hoping to buy herself some valuable time.

"Leave her, she's fine."

"But..."

"I said leave her. Do you want me to do the same thing to you?"

Pem shrugged in bewilderment as she turned around to follow Eddy. She thought that maybe Cora could run to the house and tell her mother what was going down, but apparently Eddy had read her mind.

"Don't even think about running off and telling your mommies. If the two of you aren't standing right here when we get back, there's going to be trouble, understand?" he snapped, glaring at Leah and Cora. They both nodded at him numbly.

Leah and Cora were both shaking their heads numbly as Pem followed him down the street to his house. None of them had any idea what Eddy had in store for her, but they knew it was bad.

Pem followed Eddy around to the back of his house and in through the basement door. He pulled on a string and a bare bulb illuminated the dank room which contained a washer and dryer, a dirty looking couch and chair and moldy looking boxes of Christmas decorations.

"How old are you Pem?" asked Eddy, he was standing there in front of her, he was at least five inches taller than her.

"I just turned thirteen," said Pem, her voice was shaking.

"Hmmm, much too young to be my girlfriend, but you are pretty," he said, touching her cheek.

"I don't want to be your girlfriend," snapped Pem, slapping his hand away. She was shaking uncontrollably, this was a nightmare. Eddy was evil and she had willingly walked into his lair.

"I'm thinking you really don't have a choice right now," said Eddy, flashing her a sardonic smile.

"I'm leaving," snapped Pem, spinning around and heading for the door. Eddy grabbed her by the arm and jerked her against his chest.

"I don't think you want to do that. You saw what I did to your stupid friend Leah, if you don't do exactly what I want, I'll rape your baby sister. That will mess her up real bad. You don't want that do you?"

Pem looked up into Eddy's face. She could tell, he was perfectly serious. Pem's body was shaking uncontrollably, she had never been so scared in her entire life. She wasn't quite sure what rape meant, but she had an vague idea. She had heard all the rumors about Eddy. When he got girls alone, he did bad things to them. She didn't want Eddy to do anything bad to her little sister, she was just a baby. She realized that Eddie was about to do bad things to her, but whatever he did to her, she could handle it, she was strong.

"Okay Eddy, what do you want me to do?" she sighed in resignation. The sooner she got this over with, the sooner she could get Cora home.

"The first thing is easy, I want you to touch my dick," said Eddy flashing her an evil smile and slowly unzipping his pants.

"No!" cried Pem, backing away slowly.

"Shhhh, keep your voice down, my dad is sleeping. He works nights. Remember, you said whatever I want," he told her, his voice was low and steady.

"I'll scream," said Pem, taking another step backward.

"No you won't, you already promised to do whatever I want. If you break your promise I will make you sorry. If you scream and wake my dad up, I'll hurt your sister bad. Maybe

not today, but sometime soon, you can't watch her 24 hours a day and neither can your parents. We have a deal. You promised...whatever I want."

Pem swallowed and took a tentative step toward him, she'd do just about anything to keep him from hurting her sister. He nodded to her in encouragement as he reached down and took it out. Pem didn't really want to look at it, but she was curious. It was hanging there limply, it didn't look too intimidating. She reached out gingerly, touched it, then jerked her hand away.

"Nice try, but that's not what I want. You have to play with it, make me feel good. Come here, closer," he beckoned.

"I...I, don't think I can," gasped Pem, it took all the courage she had to just touch it, she didn't think there was anyway possible she could do what he wanted.

"Sure you can."

Pem was shaking as she took a nervous step toward him. He took her hand and guided it toward him.

"You never touched one, have you?"

Pem shook her head nervously.

"Don't worry, I'll show you how to make a guy very happy."

She could feel him growing in her hand as he forced her to wrap her fingers around him, Pem pulled away nervously, this was just weird.

"No, don't stop, Pem. You promised, this is what you have to do. You don't want me to hurt your baby sister, do you?"

"No," said Pem, letting him place her hand back on his rapidly growing penis. He showed her how to move her hand, letting him set the rhythm as he taught her how he wanted to be touched. In a matter of minutes he had her hand moving faster and he was grunting and moaning like he was in pain. Pem thought she was hurting him, but he wouldn't let her stop. She was scared, she wasn't sure what was wrong with him, in a moment he shot white liquid all over her hand, as his face contorted in agony.

Pem was distressed, she didn't know what she had done to him, but she was sure he was going to be completely pissed.

"I'm sorry," cried Pem, glancing around the room nervously. She wanted to run away, but he would come after her and hurt her, she knew he would.

"No, you don't understand, that was good. I liked it, that's why I came. You ever see a guy cum before?" asked Eddy.

Pem shook her head nervously, she had no idea what he was talking about, but at least he wasn't pissed. He handed her a towel off the dryer so she could wipe off her hands.

She wiped her hands self consciously. Eddy was tucking himself back into his pants, Pem was hoping this meant he was done with her.

"Can I go?" she asked, her voice was hopeful, but she got the feeling probably not.

"Not yet," said Eddy, flashing her a sly smile.

Pem shivered nervously She wondered what else Eddy wanted from her. She was sure whatever came next would be even more humiliating. She anxiously wondered if Leah and her sister were still waiting in the street for her.

"You will do what I say Pem, and you will never tell anyone about this, do I make myself perfectly clear?"

Pem was standing there staring at him numbly. He was evil, perfectly evil.

"Promise me, promise me you will never tell, or I will do the very same thing to your baby sister."

Pem sighed, what choice did she have?

"Okay, I won't tell."

"Take your clothes off, I want to see you naked," said Eddy.

Pem sighed miserably. It seemed as if her humiliation was going to be complete. It took a while, she was wearing so many layers, but soon she was standing there shivering and naked in the cool basement as Eddy stood there looking her up and down.

"Well I guess there is not much to see. You're just plain skinny. You don't even fuckin have boobs yet," he complained, taking a bold step toward her.

"Sorry to disappoint you, are you done?" snapped Pem, rolling her eyes.

"I am nowhere near done bitch, all I care about is your tight little pussy anyway, lay on the sofa," said Eddy, pointing to an old couch covered with a tattered quilt in the corner of the room.

"Eddy please...don't do this."

"I told you, it's my turn to touch you. Lay down," said Eddy.

Pem walked over and laid on the couch, her body was shaking uncontrollably as Eddy laid down next to her.

"You ever let a guy touch your pussy before?"

Pem couldn't speak, she just shook her head nervously.

"Yeah, I thought not. Well you're gonna like it, I guarantee," said Eddy, flashing her an arrogant smile.

Pem cringed as Eddy slid his hand down between her legs, she felt the urge to clamp her legs together, but they had a deal, she would let him touch her.

Eddy slid his fingers between the soft folds between her legs and began massaging her. At first it was weird but soon he was touching a magical spot that seemed to make her begin to writhe uncontrollably. She wasn't sure if this new sensation could be considered pleasure or pain, she'd never experienced anything like this before. Eddy had closed his eyes and was breathing heavily as he kept moving his fingers quickly and deftly. Pem wasn't sure what was happening, but her breathing was speeding up as well. Without warning, Eddy plunged a finger inside her and Pem had to clamp her mouth closed so she wouldn't scream.

"Eddy stop please," she breathed.

"Sorry but I love tight little virgin pussies."

Eddy was panting, his face was beaded with sweat. He determinedly plunged two fingers inside her, causing her to writhe with a strange sensation that wasn't pain, but it was causing her body to shake uncontrollably. What was happening?

The shaking continued as Eddy rolled on top of her.

"Now I'm going to show you how big girls like to play," said Eddy.

"No!" cried Pem, suddenly realizing what Eddy had in mind.

The basement door was suddenly flung open with a crash and in seconds Pem realized that Fortuno was there. He flung Eddy across the room as if he weighed nothing at all.

Eddy was now laying in a disheveled pile in the corner of the room, moaning miserably. Fortuno came to Pem and placed his hand tenderly on her cheek.

"Get dressed and go home. I will take care of Eddy," said Fortuno.

"If I don't do what he wants, he'll hurt Cora."

"That will not be an issue, I promise you," said Fortuno, he nodded to her in encouragement.

Pem was still shaking as she struggled to get dressed. She was worried that Eddy would just come after her later, either that or he would take out his revenge with her sister.

Pem pulled her coat on and ran out of the basement and back to the street. Leah and Cora were still standing precisely where she had left them. They looked completely shocked to see her running up the hill toward them.

"Oh my God, are you okay?" cried Leah, running to her.

"I'm okay," said Pem, but she was still shaking uncontrollably as Leah hugged her.

"Oh my God, what did he do to you?" Did he hurt you?" cried Leah.

"Not bad, I'm okay," said Pem, her voice broke as she spoke. She wanted to break down in tears, but the tears wouldn't come.

"Are you sure? What did he do?"

"Don't ask me, I can't tell you. He made me promise," breathed Pem. Just saying those words made her face turn red with embarrassment.

"Oh God Pem, did he make you touch his dick?" cried Leah.

"Leah!" cried Pem, her voice raising in embarrassment. Her little sister was standing right there!

"Cora, be a good girl and go on home, I need to talk to your sister," said Leah, waving her away.

"I wanna know what happened," whined Cora.

"He made me touch his boy parts, and that's all," snapped Pem. "Now go home, and don't even think about telling mom. He'll mess us up real good if we tattle."

Cora nodded in agreement and headed up the driveway to the house.

"You have to tell me. What else did he do?" cried Leah excitedly.

"Nothing, that was it," lied Pem.

"Are you sure? You were gone for a long time. When he got Andrea Howell alone one time, he made her put it in her mouth, she gagged till she threw up," said Leah.

"Ewww, no it was nothing like that," said Pem.

"Did he touch you? My mom says he's a total pervert, he tries crap like that with girls all the time."

"No, he didn't touch me, he just made me touch him."

"That's it, then he just let you go? That doesn't sound right. I mean Pem, I've heard the stories about him. He's mean. How did you get away without him doing **something** to you?"

Pem was still shaking, still thinking about what he almost did to her. He would have too, if if wasn't for Fortuno. Where did he come from and how did he know she was in trouble?

"His dad woke up," said Pem.

Pem knew it would be the only thing that would end this awkward conversation. She could never tell Leah the truth, it was too embarrassing.   Besides, the less she knew the better. Pem just hoped she wouldn't run into Eddy again, she knew once he set his mind on something he would never let it go. She knew it was only a matter of time before they came face to face again. He lived across the the street and three houses down, this was a nightmare!

CHAPTER THREE

Pem went home and drank hot chocolate in front of the fireplace with Cora. Cora was a good sister. She never said another word about sledding or Eddy.

It snowed all night dumping another 4 inches on top of the nine they already had. Once again, school was called off and it was another perfect day to go sledding, but Pem had no desire to go out there. Eddy would be out there, and she had no desire to face Eddy.

Pem was in her room reading when the phone rang, she could hear her mother in the kitchen talking to someone.

"Oh that's awful. I admit, I have never cared for him, but still that's so sad for his family."

Pem walked to the doorway, something was up, she could hear it in her mother's voice.

"What's the matter?" asked Pem, when her mother had hung up the phone.

"That was Mrs. Morris across the street. You know Eddy Grainger from down the street right?"

Pem cringed, and resisted the urge to curse like a sailor. If he had told the neighbors what she had done, she would die!

"He's dead."

"Dead?" whispered Pem, that didn't even seem possible.

"Apparently, he ran into a tree with his sled and broke his neck," said her mother frowning.

"Broke his neck?" gasped Pem.

"Yes, isn't that horrible?"

It was horrible, for his father she supposed, but Pem almost sighed in relief. He was bad person, he'd been that way ever since she could remember. Her mother had told her it was because he had to grow up without a mother. It didn't matter, as far as Pem was concerned, it was what he deserved. Then she had a terrifying thought. Fortuno had been there in Eddy's basement. Had he done this?

Pem still wasn't sure, was Fortuno real, or was he just the subject of a strange recurring dream? Every time she saw him, it seemed there was some logical explanation for what had happened. Had he really showed up at Eddy's house yesterday? Had he killed Eddy and somehow staged it to look like an accident?

She hadn't seen Fortuno since the night she had went to his castle and that had all been explained away as a dream. If he truly was real, why didn't he come around any other times, and how had he known she was in trouble?

"I'm going over to Leah's," said Pem, she suddenly had to talk to Leah, to see what she thought.

"Okay, but no sledding today though. I'm a little freaked out right now," said her mother.

"Yeah, me too," said Pem, almost shivering at the thought.

Leah just lived up the street, her's was the white stucco house at the very top of the hill. Pem rang the doorbell and when Leah saw her standing there she immediately burst into tears.

"Did you hear what happened!" she cried.

"Yeah, totally weird, huh?

"Come on in," said Leah, motioning for Pem to follow her. They went to her room and closed the door.

"I feel awful, it's all my fault," sniffled Leah, she seemed like she was on the verge of breaking down in tears again.

"What's your fault?" asked Pem, slightly confused.

"That Eddy died. I hated him, I really did Pem. I was so upset last night that before I went to bed, I prayed that he would die. Now he's dead!"

"It's not your fault. I'm not sure, but I think it must have happened late yesterday afternoon, after we all went home. Besides, I'm sure plenty of people have prayed for that dirtbag to die."

"He was just so mean. I just wanted him to die, so he couldn't hurt anyone anymore. I was worried that he had done other things to you, things that you would feel like you needed to keep secret from me."

"There was nothing else Leah, I told you everything."

"Pem, my older sister Amy tells me everything, she knows stuff, she's fifteen. She's heard all the stories. He's done stuff to plenty of other girls. He forced them to do things they'll never live down."

"He was just a big jerk," snapped Pem, she didn't want to think of what he would have done, if Fortuno hadn't showed up.

"No, he's a freaking pervert, my sister says there is something seriously wrong with him. She wanted me to ask you if he raped you. Do you know what that means? If he raped you, you need to tell someone. You might be pregnant."

"I already told you, he didn't rape me!"

"Are you sure? Do you even know what it means?

"Not exactly, but I'm sure it's really bad! I mean if his dad hadn't woke up..."

"Do you want to talk to Amy? If you told her what he did to you, she would know if it was bad or not."
"It was bad, but he didn't get to do what he wanted..."

"Please Pem, just tell me what he did. You were gone a long time. I know he did more than just make you touch his dick."

"I can't Leah! The whole thing just totally creeped me out!"

"I'm just worried about you, what if he has like, VD or something?"

"Ewww!"

"Well he might, how would we know?"

"Leah, I really can't say the words," said Pem, her face was hot and flushed.

"How about if I ask you questions and you just answer them?"

"I guess that's okay," said Pem, though she was still so embarrassed, she felt like the might pass out.

"Did he touch you...down there?"

"Yes."

"Did he put his fingers inside you?"

Pem cringed, this was so embarrassing. "Yes."

"Did he stick his dick in there?"

"No!"

"He tried though didn't he?"

Pem started crying, she had never been so scared in her whole life. Had Fortuno really been there, or had that been a figment of her imagination?

"It's okay. As long as he didn't put his dick in you it's all good."

"Really?"

"If he did that's rape, and the stupid horny bastard would go to jail."

"He told me if I didn't do what he wanted he would rape Cora. I couldn't let him do that, I could't," sobbed Pem, she couldn't stop crying.

"I still don't get it, how did you get away?"

"His dad woke up," lied Pem, she didn't know what else to tell Leah, she would never believe that some guy named Fortuno, who was destined to be her husband someday, had come out of nowhere and saved her.

"Thank God," said Leah, hugging her.

"You're not going to tell on me, are you?"

"Why would I tell? You didn't do anything wrong."

"But..."

"You were bullied Pem. You were so brave, people do what they have to do. You saved my life, don't ever think any of that was your fault. I'm just glad that you're okay."

Pem hugged Leah, happy that she had such an understanding friend. It was true, she did what she had to do, she would never have to face Eddy Grainger again.

CHAPTER FOUR

Time seemed to pass quickly, it wasn't long before Pem was in high school. She was growing into a beautiful young woman. She loved sports and everyone was always amazed by her speed.

Her freshman year a friend talked her into trying out for the track team. She was an instant success. There wasn't a race she couldn't win. It was only a matter of time before she had a large collection of ribbons and medals.

She had finished her homework and just turned out her light when she heard a familiar voice in her room.

"Do not be afraid my darling, it is I, Fortuno," said the voice.

"May I turn the light on so that I can see you?" asked Pem. She was beginning to think she had a very overactive imagination.

"Please, leave the light out. You are growing so beautiful every day. I cannot bare to see you, knowing it will still be three years till we will marry."

"You still haven't asked me, what if I were to say no," teased Pem.

"You cannot say no to your destiny, besides, you have the mark, soon you will lust for me as much as I lust for you."

"The mark?"

"On your neck. I gave it to you the very first night we met. Whether you realized it or not, it sealed our fate. I am a vampire and the mark is my bite, I have tasted your blood

and you now have a tiny bit of the venom of a vampire running through your veins. Your transformation has already begun, when we marry, you too will be a vampire."

"I will be a vampire? I may be young and naive, but even I don't believe that crazy story," said Pem, shaking her head miserably.

"You do not believe that I am a vampire?"

"I do not believe you are a vampire, but I do believe you are batty."

"Eddy's death was not an accident," said, Fortuno.

Pem gasped, somehow she knew it, but the thought didn't seem real.

"Did you kill Eddy?"

"You already know I did."

"How did you get into my room?"asked Pem, her heart was suddenly pounding uneasily.

"The same way I always get in, I have powers, I can be anywhere I need to be in a mere moment."

"Why are you here?" asked Pem. She was suddenly frightened.

"Since you attracted the attention of the very naughty, horny young boy, I have felt the need to keep a closer eye on you lately. We are to be married, you are my beautiful flower, I will not have mere mortals drooling over you."

Pem couldn't help it, she giggled. This was the most ridiculous thing she had ever heard.

"So would you say you are here in my room every night?"

"Yes, I would say that."

"Have you nothing better to do than to watch me sleep?"

"Since you have turned fifteen I have watched you constantly, in your sleep, at school, walking home with your friends. I am patiently waiting for your eighteenth birthday, and protecting you in the meantime."

"Protecting me? Yes, what did you do to Eddy?"

"I broke the horny bastard's neck. I know exactly what he was planning to do to you. Forgive me for being so jealous, but I cannot help it, you are mine."

"I guess I don't understand, how is it that I came to be betrothed to a vampire?" asked Pem.

"You are the first born daughter of Ludmilla, a blood princess of our clan. Your mother is of our clan's noblest blood. She has many powers, but she left our kingdom. She shunned her ties to the clan to marry a mortal. She was betrothed to the great King Vitale, but she did not love him."

"Wait a minute, are you telling me that my mother is a vampire?"

"Yes of course, though by marrying a mortal, she can never ascend to the throne. You, her firstborn daughter are betrothed to me and we will restore the rightful power to our coven."

"What happened to King Vitale, did he marry another?"

"His love for Ludmilla was intense. On the night of their wedding she caused a huge scandal and refused him. The poor King died later that evening, I've been told he died of a broken heart. The kingdom mourned and soon began to splinter after his death. Our marriage will restore the crown to it's rightful reign, which will in turn, restore faith to our kind."

"What if I refuse to marry you?"

"You cannot, it is your destiny. Besides, why would you do such a thing?" asked Fortuno, moving out of the shadows to be closer to her. She could see his luminous skin in the moonlight. He looked truly beautiful.

"Perhaps I want to marry for love, like my mother," said Pem, she was teasing him a bit, it wasn't in her nature to just go along quietly.

"You already love me, my precious flower," said Fortuno, gently placing his hand on her cheek.

"Really? I'm not sure I believe you."

Fortuno took her face in his hands and kissed her. The kiss started out gentle, but as his lips caressed hers Pem could feel her heart accelerating and as soon as his tongue touched her lips, Pem felt her own lips parting and the kiss grew deeper and more passionate. When he finally released her she was gasping to breathe.

"Are you convinced of our love yet, Pemberthy Louise Parker?"

"Not yet, kiss me some more," she breathed, giving him a shy smile.

"I do not think that is a good idea."

"Must we stop?" she breathed, reaching for him in the darkness. She didn't want to stop, she felt as if a fire had been ignited within her body. It was the most delicious feeling she had ever felt.

"We must, I may be immortal, but like most men, there are certain things that make me weak. You my darling, are one of my weaknesses."

"You really love me?"

"I love you more than anything, and now my body wants you as well, but I must wait."

"Why must we wait?" asked Pem, for the first time in her life she felt as if she needed more. In fact, it felt as if her entire body was on fire. His kiss had awakened something inside her and now she only wanted the fire to be quenched. Her desire was suddenly overwhelming.

"There is a time for everything my darling. We must wait for your powers to mature, to take you now would only satisfy our lust, if we wait our powers will be much stronger."

"What powers?"

"You will have many, but you must learn to be more discreet. If the world were to know of your powers it would be dangerous for you. As you've realized, you are fast, much faster than any normal mortal. You must stop racing, do not draw attention to yourself. You put your life in danger."

"But how do I put myself in danger?"

"Ours is but one clan among vampires. There are others that wish to destroy us. You are destined to be our Queen, it would be easy now, while you are so young and your powers

are undeveloped. If your true identity was found out by a rival clan, they might seek to destroy you," said Fortuno.

Pem shivered, she'd never thought that her life might be in danger.

"Do not worry. I will always be here to protect you. You should do your best to keep your abilities under wraps, it is just safer that way."

"Fortuno?"

"Yes, my love?"

"Will you hold me?"

Fortuno moved closer and folded her into his arms. As she lay there in his arms in her bed Pem thought she had never felt safer in her life. She snuggled against his chest and kissed him lightly.

Fortuno wrapped his arms around her and kissed her passionately. Pem was delighted with his response, she kissed him back, pressing her body shyly against his. Pem felt the light touch of his teeth on her neck and she was almost gasping with pleasure. He pulled away from her abruptly.

"No Fortuno, don't stop. Bite me...I know you want to."

He had jumped up and was standing beside the bed gasping and stepping away carefully.

"You don't know what you are asking for, we must wait."

"You want me and I want you. You want to bite me, and you want to make love to me."

"I have already given you a small bite, the bite that binds you to me. Our love will grow and you will want me as much as I want you. We cannot do what our bodies demand of us, it is coven law that we wait till you turn eighteen.

Once I bite you again, it will be forever, there will be no turning back. Once I taste your blood again I will not be satisfied until I drain every drop of your blood and you will be a vampire forever."

"I don't care, I don't want to wait anymore," breathed Pem, her heart was pounding and her body was on fire. She didn't know how they could possibly wait three more years.

"You must put the needs of the coven above the needs of the flesh. We will be magnificent together, but we must wait, you will see my darling," said Fortuno. With that he kissed her hand and disappeared into thin air.

Pem tried to calm the furious beating of her heart. She had never wanted anything so badly in her life. What sort of magic did this man possess, that his kisses made her feel as if she were going to burst into flames?

Could she possibly wait three more years for this man? It hardly seemed likely.

R. J. HANRAHAN

CHAPTER FIVE

Sweet sixteen and never been kissed, though that sure didn't seem to apply to Pem. She did her best to behave like a normal teenage girl at school, but at night she just couldn't help herself knowing that Fortuno was there in her room watching her.

Sometimes he would get into bed with her and kiss her, but Pem was getting bored with the kisses and the light petting they enjoyed. She was suddenly determined to have more, she wanted Fortuno to quench the fire that he had created within her, she wanted him to make love to her, she felt as if she couldn't stand it another moment.

"Fortuno, come to me tonight and kiss me," said Pem as she lay there in her bed. She had not seen him, but she knew he was there.

"I cannot as I fear I will not be able to stop myself, my body aches for you my darling."

"I don't know what you've done to me but I can't stand it anymore. I want you to make love to me."

"I fear when I bit you, you may have got too much venom. You are supposed to desire me, but not so much, so soon. I'm sorry, we must wait my darling, our time will come," said his voice, though he refused to make himself visible to her.

"I **do** desire you Fortuno, I can't stop thinking about it. I want to feel you inside of me," whined Pem.

"Do you see why I cannot risk being in your bed tonight. Just the thought of you and your dirty talk has given me a raging hard on."

"May I touch it?" asked Pem, smiling to herself. She knew if she touched him, he wouldn't be able to stop and finally this fire that was burning inside her would be quenched.

"Absolutely not! If you were to touch me, I doubt I could stop. I'm not sure what's gotten into you, you're so horny, yet you are just sixteen. I can barely wait until your eighteenth birthday, I will definitely have my hands full with you."

"Please Fortuno, I just want to touch it."

"I'm not sure I trust you, what if you were to seduce me?"

"What if?" giggled Pem.

"Sorry my Lady, but you are just too young."

"I touched Eddy's cock, he seemed to like it," teased Pem, she was trying to make him jealous.

"I know, I'm trying to forget."

"I jacked him off, he came all over my hand," breathed Pem. She hated to think about it, but perhaps Fortuno would be so jealous, he would just relent.

"He touched me too," sighed Pem languorously stretching her body out in the bed.

"Pem, please..."

"Fortuno, I want you to touch me."

"No."
"Perhaps if I am naked you will not be able to resist me," giggled Pem, striping off her pajamas and throwing them out from underneath the covers.

"The answer is no."

"If you won't touch me, I guess I will have to touch myself," said Pem, running her hands slowly across her breasts.

"Do as you wish, my will is stronger than my desire."

"Look how hard my nipples get when I touch them, but your tongue would feel so much better, don't you want me?"

"I can play these games with you all night, of course I want you darling, but we can't. It is the law of the coven."

Pem felt compelled by a force she couldn't control, her entire body was on fire and she just wanted Fortuno to make love to her, and extinguish the raging flames. It was as if some sort of spell had been placed on her mind and her body, she would not stop till he gave in.

She slid her hands down her stomach to touch herself. Her fingers parted her hair and slid into the wet folds. She couldn't see him, but she hoped Fortuno was watching her as she worked her fingers slowly at first, then her pace increased feverishly until she felt her hips bucking involuntarily and a broken moan escaped her lips.

"Oh please Fortuno," she moaned.

"Damn it, you're killing me!" cried Fortuno, who had suddenly appeared in her bed.

He gathered her in his ams and kissed her passionately, he ran his hands over her breasts eagerly as Pem sighed contentedly.

Pem had already decided there was no way she could possibly wait two more years. She wanted Fortuno tonight, and she was going to have him. She pressed her body

against his and kissed him passionately, feeling his growing passion pressing against her abdomen.

Fortuno kissed her neck, his kisses followed the curve of her neck to her breast. Pem's heart was pounding hard as he took her nipple into his mouth, causing Pem to gasp with pleasure.

Pem was so excited she wanted to touch him, she ran her hands down the length of his muscular torso. His body was so magnificently strong and alluring. She was inexperienced, but she still remembered what had happened when she touched Eddy Grainger's dick, it had grown hard as a rock almost instantly. If she hadn't been so repulsed by Eddy himself, she would have found it very fascinating.

She wanted to find out if she could have the same effect on Fortuno. Pem's hands were sneaking lower, to the soft shock of curly pubic hair that surrounded her intended target. She boldly wrapped her fingers around his already swollen manhood. Fortuno gasped with pleasure. Pem couldn't help but smile. It was hard as a rock and probably twice as large as Eddy's. Pem knew, guys couldn't help but brag about how big they were, she had never understood the bragging before, now she finally got it. Apparently men's penises were like some kind of trophy. It was completely mind boggling that she seemed to have a sort of control over him.

"Pem please, we must stop. Have you any idea what you are doing to me?" he moaned breathlessly.

"Fortuno, I don't understand, why must we wait? If you want me so badly why can't we just do it now?"

"The laws of our coven dictate that you must be eighteen, a mature woman in the eyes of the council."

"If you'll just touch me, you'll see how mature I am. Pleasure Fortuno, I don't want to wait anymore."

"I want nothing more but..."

"Two years is a very long time," said Pem, guiding his hand down between her legs so that he could feel how wet she was. Now that she had felt how much he wanted her, it seemed as if she couldn't stop herself.

Fortuno gasped when Pem guided his hand between her legs, he wanted to touch her so bad, but he was afraid, his desire was so strong, he knew he wouldn't be able to stop. What would the courts do to him if he broke the laws of the coven and joined with Pem before they were married? It could be considered treason, a crime punishable by death.

His body was overpowering his mind, his fingers could not resist the warm wetness between Pem's legs, she was ready and so was he, he couldn't stop his fingers from exploring. Pem responded with bucking hips and sighs of pleasure. He wanted nothing more but to give her exactly what she wanted so badly.

Pem rolled on top of him and wedged her nipple in his mouth, he sucked greedily on it as he dipped three fingers into her warm wetness, Pem shuddered and gasped.

"Please Fortuno, I want to feel you inside me."

"The Council will have my head. I'm not quite sure what they would do to me."

"How could they possibly know? Please Fortuno, I want you to make love to me,"cried Pem, kissing him passionately.

"There will be no turning back Pem, you're sure?" he slid his fingers into her again, as Pem bucked against him moaning in ecstasy.

"I'm ready, please don't make me wait anymore."

Fortuno could wait no longer either, he moved on top of her finally sliding into her warm, welcoming wetness. Pem shuddered uncontrollably as he moved inside her. Fortuno's fangs punctured her neck at the same time she finally lost her virginity. He made love to her as he sucked every last bit of blood from her body and she clung to him, her body shuddering with the most intense orgasm he had ever seen. She was finally his, the Queen of the Coven.

CHAPTER SIX

When Pem awoke, she was there in the castle. She felt fabulous. In fact, she had never felt so good in her entire life. Fortuno had finally made love to her, and as promised, it had been magnificent. When he finally came inside her it was the most intense pleasure she had ever experienced in her entire life.

She finally felt complete, this was her destiny. She felt a little guilty for seducing him like that, but she told herself, there was absolutely no reason to wait another two years for that. Just like she had dreamed, it had been perfect. Now she was here in her castle, married to Fortuno and she would be the Queen of their coven.

Pem was ravenously hungry. Not for food so much, but she had an overwhelming taste for blood. She looked down and noticed that her skin had a pale translucent glow. That's when she realized exactly what had happened last night. Not only had Fortuno made love to her, but he had bitten her as well. She didn't remember anything after that, but obviously she was no longer human, she had made the transition. She was a vampire now and her body wanted blood.

Pem ambled to the door of her room and opened it, there was a servant right outside the door. The woman looked startled to see her at first.

"My Queen," said the woman, bowing regally to her.

"I need blood," cried Pem, her thirst was so intense, she resisted the overwhelming urge to sink her teeth into this nervous little servant girl.

In what seemed like only an instant, Fortuno appeared at her side. He took both her hands in his and looked into her eyes.

"Are you well my darling?" he asked, his face full of concern.

"I am so thirsty," she whined. The servant girl had scurried away, but momentarily, a man in full castle livery appeared with carafe and a goblet.

"My Queen," he said, pouring the blood into the goblet and holding it out to her.

Pem grabbed the goblet greedily and drank it down. It tasted amazing and she began to feel better almost immediately.

"Ahh, the bane of our existence, our need for blood," said Fortuno, with a slight frown.

"Shall it eclipse my need for you?" asked Pem, seductively kissing his hand.

"Hopefully, nothing will eclipse your need for me."

Pem smiled at him and led him to her bed. It was strange, her transformation had left her strong, energetic and strangely insatiable.

Pem couldn't seem to quench her desire for her new husband even though she knew the two of them had already achieved their goal. Their offspring had been conceived the night of the first coupling. Pem was sure of it. She had felt her tiny baby burning inside of her from the moment of it's conception. Within hours she had felt it moving and turning inside her. This child would be royalty and Pem couldn't wait to see the beautiful result of her lovemaking with Fortuno, it would, no doubt, be the most beautiful baby in the world.

After they made love, Fortuno held her in his arms and she snuggled against his hard body. Pem felt as if she had died and gone to heaven she felt so happy. How could life be any better? She was married to the most gorgeous man she had ever met and their child would one day be King. Pem didn't think anything could ever bring her down from this high.

I fear I must meet with the council later," Fortuno told her, his voice was grim.

"Are we in trouble?" asked Pem. She almost shuddered as she thought about what Fortuno had told her. It was coven law that the Queen be at least eighteen. She was just sixteen, yet she had undergone her transformation and she was certain she was now carrying their heir inside her. The council would be rightly upset.

"Well, I am in trouble I imagine. The council will forgive you as you will be considered too young to be responsible for our unfortunate lapse in judgement," said Fortuno, frowning slightly.

"But I was fully responsible. It wasn't really a bad thing. I'm ready, I'm carrying our child Fortuno, the future King, how can they find that so wrong? Besides, it was all my fault, you were trying to be obedient. I just couldn't wait any longer, I didn't mean to get you into trouble," cried Pem, she was suddenly upset.

"I know my love. What's done is done. With any luck we have conceived a Prince and the council will overlook my lack of self control and give me some sort of lesser punishment."

"What sort of punishment are you facing?"

"Well, I imagine it depends on how much I've angered the council."

"May I go to the council?"

"No my darling. You've only just turned. You're going to need blood, and lots of it. It's best that you stay in our chambers for now. Besides you will not be allowed to testify in my behalf, you are only sixteen, not yet an adult in the eyes of the court."

"But I want to go," said Pem, pouting.

"You will listen to me for once and stay here. If the council is quite angry, your presence there will only make things worse."

Pem nodded her head in resignation, she'd already caused enough trouble for him. She'd practically seduced him in her own bedroom. When it was over and Fortuno realized what he had done, he was frantic. They had rushed back to the castle to be married by the coven minister, in a desperate effort to make things right in the eyes of the council.

Fortuno wasn't as naive as Pem was. He knew the laws and he also knew the penalties for breaking those laws. He was worried. The council would be extremely upset that he had jumped the gun by nearly two years and taken his wife before her eighteenth birthday. He wondered what sort of punishment he might be facing. The council didn't like it when members of the clan disobeyed their ancient laws, especially a coven member as high ranking as he was.

Fortuno went to the great hall to meet with the council. Marble and gold leaf touched every surface of the candle lit great hall. He had dressed in his finest purple tunic in an effort to reinforce to the council his high rank within the

coven. Surely they would take mercy on him since he was destined to restore the coven to it's former glory.

The council members were already ensconced behind the heavy wood table that curved in a half circle in front of him.

The council, all dressed in heavy burgundy colored cloaks assessed him carefully as he approached. Their faces were not even visible beneath their hoods in the shadowy candle light. Fortuno took a slow deep breath in an attempt to calm his frazzled nerves. A tense silence had engulfed the room, the tension was so thick, you could cut it with a knife.

The council member at the center of the table suddenly cleared his throat and rose to his feet to address Fortuno.

"Welcome Fortuno. We have gathered today to address complaints that you overstepped your authority within the clan and broke ancient coven law. You have brought Pemberthy Parker here and made her your bride nearly two years before her eighteenth birthday. What say you, Fortuno?"

"Forgive me Councilman, but may I ask who initiated the complaint?" asked Fortuno.

"It does not matter who initiated the complaint, you have broken the law, have you not?"

"I admit that I have broken the law, but no harm is done. I simply want to know who filed the formal complaint," he sighed.

"The complainant is her mother, Ludmilla."

"Is her objection to me, or to the timeliness of our marriage?"

"It makes no difference, this entire fiasco is unheard of. You are not authorized to go over our heads and shatter tradition simply because you cannot control your wanton sexual urges!" snapped the councilman, his voice raising in anger.

"Councilman I agree, I was weak, but it is not entirely my fault. My will is strong, but hers is stronger. I tried to resist her, but...I'm not really sure what happened. I dare say she will make an excellent Queen when she comes of age."

"I couldn't agree more Fortuno. Unfortunately, her mother is very angry about the entire situation. She claims the girl is too young to take the throne and therefore too young to produce an heir. She alleges that you seek to control her daughter and have used her specifically to ascend to the throne."

"Poppycock! Pem is perfectly capable of taking the throne, and I am certain she is already carrying our heir. What does her mother propose that we do at this point?" asked Fortuno, his voice bordering on sarcasm.

"She wants the marriage annulled immediately and her daughter placed in seclusion until the baby is born."

"Seclusion! That's completely mad! Pem is the clan's new queen," cried Fortuno.

"Not officially, there has been no coronation. There has been a serious breech of protocol. When the rest of the coven finds out what has happened there could be discord among our members. We want to unite our clan, not cause it to splinter even further. Our coven's future has not been so dire since the death of King Vitale. If we allow these antics to go unpunished we might face a rebellion. That is a possibility we cannot risk.

"Rebellion! By who?"

"My poor dear Fortuno, had you spent more time studying, and less time obsessing over your beautiful bride you would know that there is a very large portion of the coven that feels the lines of power should return to the line of Milan. If Ludmilla were to have her way, your betrothal would have never happened in the first place. Ludmilla would have her daughter marry into the Milan line."

"And marry who? The only viable candidate would be Salinar. He's a complete ass, Pem would never be compatible with him!"

"In case you haven't realized, this is not so much about compatibility, as it is about politics. King Vitale thought he had exacted his revenge by betrothing the girl to you, perhaps Ludmilla will win after all. Being just sixteen years old, the girl is still the ward of her mother. As far as this court sees it, the baby, if there is one, will fall under the custody of Pemberthy's mother," said the speaker of the court."

"Wait a minute, are you saying that my mother in law will get custody of **my** child, the heir to the throne?" cried Fortuno.

"Yes, of course."

"But what about my rights? I fathered the child," snapped Fortuno.

"How is this court to know that you didn't seduce this poor child just to obtain an heir, you knew she was too young, yet..."

"I swear to this court, this wasn't premeditated. I love Pem with all my heart. Of course I desired her, but it was as if she desired me even more than I desired her. I tried to resist, but it was impossible. I fear that when I gave her that small bite as a child, she got too much venom."

"My noble prince, are denying that you made love to this child?"

"No sir," breathed Fortuno.

"During your lovemaking, did you not drain every drop of blood from her body, to sustain your own?"

"I did, I did, but.."

"Fortuno of Urbino, we have found you guilty of crimes against the clan, defying the traditions of the crown and essentially committing treason," the speaker of the court's voice echoed throughout the courtroom.

"No, no, that's all wrong," cried Fortuno. He was suddenly panicking.

"I believe you know the penalty for treason," said the speaker, flashing him an evil smile.

"Please your excellency. I have done nothing wrong. I love her. We have produced a legal heir. The next King of our coven," cried Fortuno.

"Fortuno of Milan, this court has ordered that you be burned in the courtyard for your crimes, with the kingdom to witness."

Fortuno fell brokenly to his knees, his grief was so overwhelming.

"What will happen to my wife?"

"This court has decided your fate, it shall determine hers as well. Guards, please take him to the tower." snapped the speaker.

Fortuno was terrified. The guards were taking him by the arms to lead him away, he worried his fate and that of his wife was already decided, and it was not favorable.

"Please your excellency, show some mercy to us, my wife is so young, I fear I have ruined everything for us."

"As I said, you will await your fate in the tower." snapped the speaker, as they dragged Fortuno forcibly from the court.

CHAPTER SEVEN

Pem was nervously pacing around her room, Fortuno had been called away to the Governing council. He had been apprehensive, Pem was nervous too. What would she do if anything happened to Fortuno?

She could feel her baby kicking inside her abdomen and her abdomen had already begun to swell slightly. She knew that women were usually pregnant for nine months, but there was no way she could possibly be growing like this for nine months. Obviously, vampire babies grew very fast.

Pem sighed miserably, how had she become involved in all of this and not questioned any of it for even an instant? She had willingly made herself into a vampire and now she had an almost ceaseless urge for blood. She was now realizing that if her body continued to grow so quickly, she would be giving birth to a vampire baby very soon, the very thought seemed completely irrational.

If she were to go home and tell her story to any rational person they would have her locked up in an insane asylum. Though at this point, she was beginning to realize that going home was probably not an option.

Pem was actually beginning to wonder if her life was in danger. She felt incredibly ignorant about this strange society she was now a part of. Along with her new husband Fortuno she had broke the ancient laws of their coven, ancient laws and customs she truly had no knowledge of.

Sure, there was some sort of a court and she was certain that Fortuno would be given an opportunity to argue his case, but would this ancient council, that she had no experience with, be as fair and just as the modern courts she had grown up with, or would they consider her and Fortuno

treasonous rebells who would require severe punishment, or worse...death?

Pem startled from her thoughts as the door to the room was flung open but it was not Fortuno who appeared, but her mother.

"Mother!" she cried, completely stunned to see her mother standing there in the doorway. She barely recognized her as she was completely adorned in the medieval style clothing she had seen the others in the castle attired in.

She still wasn't sure that all of this had sunk in. It hadn't been till Fortuno had came to her that she realized that her mother was not a normal mortal, but heir to this vampire coven's monarchy.

Pem had never seen her mother in this role, but she had to admit, she did look lovely. Her mother's long blond hair was braided into long ropes that were piled carefully on top of her head and the jeweled headpiece that sat upon her head seemed to confirm her noble roots. Her pale alabaster skin was only exaggerated by her sapphire silk gown which flowed around her like a delicate spring breeze.

"My dearest daughter, what have you done?" she cried, coming to Pem and gathering her into her arms.

"I have married Fortuno, I am going to have his baby." said Pem, stepping back a bit so that her mother could see her swollen abdomen. It had been but days, yet her abdomen was nearly as large as someone who was 4 months pregnant, it hardly seemed possible.

"That is why I have come, I have news for you from the council."

"What has the court said about my marriage to Fortuno?"

"The court has found your marriage invalid. You are not of age. You are too young to take on the role of Queen. The marriage will be annulled," said her mother, her voice was flat and void of any emotion.

"But, Fortuno told me..."

"I'm sorry to say it, but Fortuno was foolish and how shall I say it...overzealous. His shocking lack of self control is not only embarrassing, but the annulment of your marriage will leave your poor child a bastard.

Unfortunately, you are but sixteen, not yet capable of ruling an entire coven. You are so young and vulnerable as far as our race is concerned, it is quite possible you may not even be strong enough to withstand this pregnancy.

"What?" cried Pem. This was all so foreign for her and difficult to comprehend.

"Childbirth is different for us than it is for mortals. If by some miracle you are strong enough to make it through your entire pregnancy and childbirth, you are certainly not capable of raising the child. He will be placed in my care until you reach legal age," snapped Ludmilla.

"No, he's my baby! I will not let you take my son from me!" cried Pem, she was completely horrified.

"It is the will and the law of the coven, we truly have no choice."

Pem sighed miserably. What had happened to her life? It was only days ago she was a normal high school student with hardly a care in the world, now she was pregnant with a vampire baby and her entire life seemed to be hanging in the

balance. A vampire coven court would decide her fate. The very thought sounded ridiculous.

"I seem to be growing so fast, how long till he's born?"

"Another several weeks or so, you've done well enough so far, I'm worried about you though, I have serious doubts you can make it through childbirth, you are much too young. It's different for us than it is for mortals. Only the very strong can even survive it. I guess you could say, it's meant to weed out the weak."

"I can handle it," seethed Pem, she was angry, this child was hers, how could she possibly pass him over to her mother to raise?

"I certainly hope so," said her mother, smugly.

"Where is my husband?"

"In the tower for now. He'll be imprisoned there until a final decision on his fate is made by the council. I assume he'll burn by next week."

"Burn!"

"Why yes, that **is** the sentence for treason. I'm sorry to say that you, Pemberthy Louise Parker are the heartless vixen who drove him to it," said Ludmilla, a slight smile coming to her face.

"I drove him to it?' cried Pem.

"Well seduced him, if one believes the rumors that are flying around here."

"I..." Pem couldn't speak, she could only think back to the overwhelming need she felt for Fortuno, it was so strong,

she knew now that it could only be a spell or something. She was learning that all vampires had certain powers. Someone had controlled her mind and her body to cause her to seduce Fortuno.

But who could have possibly done such a thing? Who stood to profit from their premature coupling? Her mother, Ludmilla had a strange, arrogant smile on her face.

"Do you deny you are to blame?"

"I couldn't help it. It was like....wait, it was you. You put some sort of spell on me, you were controlling me!" cried Pem, completely horrified.

"How else was I to get control of the coven? Your betrothal was arranged years ago, I had no say in the matter. I couldn't stand by and allow the line of succession go to the Urbinos. The betrothal contract was airtight, I had to come up with another plan.

In case you haven't noticed, men are controlled by their penises. Alas, I am not capable of controlling Fortuno's mind, but you are my blood, so I can, in many cases control yours. I knew if I filled your mind with uncontrollable sexual urges you would somehow manage to seduce him and cause poor, hapless Fortuno to succumb to his desires and in the process, inadvertently commit treason.

In the grand scheme of things, Fortuno will be put to death, you will be considered too young to be a mother to the young Prince and I will have control over him and our kingdom, for the next two years at the very least," said Ludmilla, flashing her daughter an evil smile.

"Oh my God! I was nothing but a pawn in your quest for power. If you wanted to control the coven, why didn't you just marry the King when you had the chance?"

"It would have never worked out, the man was a complete moron, we didn't see eye to eye on anything. Besides, barring an annulment like I'm affording you, marriage is for eternity. Vampires don't die and they are rather hard to kill. The King had numerous lovers who all rumored him to be a very poor lover.

I guess I couldn't envision myself spending eternity married to a man who I wasn't attracted to, couldn't possibly satisfy me sexually and had absolutely nothing in common with."

"Oh mother, how impossibly shallow," snapped Pem.

"Don't judge me. I'm not the slut about to give birth to a bastard child."

"Fortuno and I are married, I love him! Are you certain he has to burn? Couldn't they show a little mercy and just imprison him?"

"He has committed treason, but perhaps they will find mercy for him since he is father of the future King."

"I don't know what I'd do if they took Fortuno away from me." sighed Pem.

"My dear, your future with Fortuno is over whether he be alive or dead. Fortuno will be imprisoned, most likely, indefinitely. You will be confined to your chambers, I'm guessing, till you turn eighteen."

"Confined to my chambers!"cried Pem.

"You've already conceived one bastard child. I doubt the council will take the chance of you conceiving another with God knows who. You are royalty my dear, we must protect your reputation."

"I already told you, my child is not a bastard! Fortuno and I are married."

"For the moment only, by this afternoon I will have the annulment papers which will make this little fiasco just like it never even happened."

Pem gasped, staring at her mother in shock, she had no idea the council would take this so seriously.

"Consider this, if Fortuno lives, you can never marry another. If he is executed, I will have you betrothed to a man of my choosing."

Pem rolled her eyes. "Who would that be?"

"Salinar Milan. The family of Milan will create a much stronger royal bloodline within the coven. When you reach the age of eighteen the two of you can be married."

"No! I will not marry this man, I love Fortuno."

"Yes, I know. All the more reason for me to push for his execution," snapped Ludmilla, spinning and heading toward the door and slamming it shut behind her.

R. J. HANRAHAN

CHAPTER EIGHT

Pem was scared. She had been locked in her chambers and she hadn't seen or heard anything from anyone in days. The only souls who came to her chambers were the servants who brought her the blood that she craved so ravenously.

Pem was grief stricken and completely alone. Her own mother had betrayed her and Fortuno, the father of her baby. The love of her life was either imprisoned in the tower, or dead. Pem shuddered to think of either possibility, but she knew, if Fortuno could have come to her, he would have by now. At this point, she really had no choice but to assume that he was dead and her fate was sealed. She was destined to be locked away in her chambers for the next two years. She also knew that as soon as she had given birth, her mother would take custody of her child.

Pem was frightened about her future and that of her baby. She wondered if the child she was carrying could even become King under the circumstances. If her mother had arranged for her marriage to Fortuno to be annulled, the child would now be considered a bastard and she was guessing that would mean there was virtually no chance of him ever becoming King.

There was a sharp rapping on the door. Pem jumped nervously. "Who is it?"

"A friend," said an unfamiliar male voice.

"You must be mistaken, I have no friends," Pem told him ruefully.

The door opened and a man stepped in. He was tall and regal looking with a sharp, angular looking face. He had

deep topaz colored eyes that were so piercing, they sent a shiver through Pem's entire body.

"My Queen," said the man, bowing regally to her.

"I am a prisoner not your Queen, please rise," snapped Pem. She was tired of this charade. She just wanted to go home, but obviously, that was completely out of the question.

The man was looking her over curiously. Pem sighed with irritation.

"Exactly what was it that you wanted?"

"For a woman exiled, you certainly are unkind to your only visitor, who is I might add, merely concerned of your well being," snapped the man, giving her a stern glare down the end of his nose.

"In case you haven't noticed, I am very pregnant and not in the best of spirits. You are my first visitor in days. Have you come to give me news on the whereabouts of my husband?"

"If you are speaking of Fortuno, I'm afraid that legally, the two of you are no longer married. More importantly, he's dead."

"Dead," whimpered Pem.

"Convicted of treason and burned, more specifically," said the man, his deep voice was void of any emotion.

Pem tried to choke back her tears, but it was impossible. She had been holding out hope that the council would spare his life, now she could hold back her tears no more.

The man held his arms open to her as she sobbed but she shook her head numbly, she didn't know this man. Why would he even offer to comfort her?

"There, there. Do not lament what is gone, look to the future, soon you will give birth to your child, our future King, or so it has been rumored."

"I have no future," snapped Pem, angrily.

"You are young, your life in this coven has just begun. Perhaps there is a better match for you."

"No there is not, Fortuno was perfect for me."

"Ahhh, from the mouth of babes. I find your naivety quite amusing. Some day you will realize, Fortuno had nothing to offer you but his stunning good looks. Someday you will realize there is much more to life than the superficial." said the man, flashing her a smile that was entirely too smug, as far a Pem was concerned.

"Who are you?" she snapped, her patience was wearing this with this uninvited visitor.

"Who would you like me to be?" he said, smiling mysteriously.

"I'm afraid I don't have the patience for these games today. I've just been informed that my husband is dead. I suddenly care not who you are. Please leave and at least, allow me to grieve his death in peace," sighed Pem, she was growing weary of her obnoxious visitor.

"How ungracious you are, your Majesty. We may have to work on your manners before your 'official' coronation. I wouldn't want to be embarrassed of you," said the man, raising his eyebrows in mock astonishment.

Pem intended to unleash a tirade on the man at this point, he was unnervingly annoying. Unfortunately, at that moment, she felt an intense pain rip through her abdomen. The onset was so abrupt and violent, she could barely make it to the nearby chair to sit down.

The man caught a glance of her stricken face and smiled.

"Ahh, it seems our Prince is finally ready to make his appearance."

"Yes," gasped Pem. The agonizing pain was almost unbearable. It had come out of nowhere and now, just moments later, she could feel her entire body succumbing to the formidable power of it.

"I must warn you, your agony has only begun. I'm afraid that vampire Princes are never very kind when they make their entrance into this world. I have no doubt you are in for a very long night."

"So I've heard," groaned Pem, wondering why this man was still here and what on Earth he wanted. The pain was searing and she felt as if she could barely breathe. She just wanted him to leave.

"Forgive me for not introducing myself sooner. My name is Salinar of Milan. If you are strong enough to live through the birth of your bastard Prince, I believe you will be interested to know that we are betrothed."

"No," breathed Pem, it was the only word she could even utter for the moment. The pain of her labor was taking up every bit of energy she had in her body.

"I'll go summon the midwife. You and I will have plenty of time to argue later, if you survive childbirth. I am rather hoping you do, you are quite pretty."

Pem didn't have a witty retort, she was doubled over in the chair, struggling merely to breathe. She had never experienced pain like this before and it was completely consuming her.

The midwife arrived and attended to her. Just when Pem thought that she couldn't make it through another body splitting contraction, the next one would arrive causing her to detest her chaotic life even more.

At some point she must have finally passed out. When she awoke, she was tucked tidily into her bed, the room was clean and dim.

Her last memory of the room was complete chaos, she'd been tangled in the blood soaked sheets, clawing at the mattress and screeching out in pain. The midwife who had been tasked with assisting in her delivery, had been more like some sort of nun, not useful to her at all. The poor frightened woman had not offered her any relief or support but spent most of her time chanting and praying, louder and louder in an attempt to drown out Pem's screams.

The room was a peaceful contrast to it's previous chaotic state. It was quiet and completely dark except for a candle on the bedside table and a large candelabra across the room. Pem was exhausted and clammy, like someone who had been sweating profusely and was now recovering.

She sat up and looked around the room, there was no one there. Salinar was gone and the midwife was gone as well. As she sat there looking around she felt the urge to touch her baby, to caress the tiny Prince she carried in her womb,

that was when she realized one other thing. She was no longer pregnant.

CHAPTER NINE

Pem was alone in her room, she hadn't seen anyone in more than a week and she was growing frightened. Would she be the next one to be executed now that she had given birth to her child? She had passed out right before the child's birth, at this point she knew not if she'd had a boy or a girl. In her heart she knew the baby had been a son, but she currently had no evidence to support that.

She tried to talk to the servants that waited upon her, but they were either incapable of speech, or sworn to silence around her because no matter how she pleaded with them, they only bowed to her in submission, none of them had spoke so much as a word to her.

Pem was beginning to fear that she would go crazy without human companionship. Just a warm voice to reassure her would have helped, but her solitary confinement drug on and on.

Early one evening there was a rap at the door as she gazed out through the bars of her prison over the moonlit hills of the kingdom she knew nothing about.

"Come in," she sighed, convinced it was nothing but another silent servant.

The door opened and in walked Salinar, of all people. He was attired completely in navy velvet with gold, jewels and white ruffles covering the front of his elaborate medieval attire. He was tall and muscular, but he was almost too severe looking to be considered handsome, but in her deprived state, Pem was finding his presence actually welcome. She just needed someone, anyone to talk to.

"What do you want?" she spat.

"A rather harsh greeting for one's fiancee, don't you think?" he asked, eyeing her playfully.

"One cannot have a fiancee, if one is already married," said Pem, narrowing her eyes at him.

"Say what you wish, but Fortuno is dead and your sham marriage has been annulled. When your two years of confinement is finally over you will be begging me to make love to you," said Salinar, flashing her an arrogant smile.

"I seriously doubt it," snapped Pem, turning away from him and gazing out the window again.

"Perhaps what you need is a few more months of solitary confinement, just to help you to yearn for my presence."

"I am guessing I will never yearn for your presence," snapped Pem, refusing to even look his direction.

Salinar stepped over to her and placed his hand on her chin, gently turning her face towards him.

"You will not only yearn for my presence, but your body will ache for me to make love to you. When we marry, we will conceive a Princess and on our marriage, your son, the Prince will become my legal son. The line of Milan will rule the entire coven and you will be the most powerful Queen of all time."

"And what about my mother? I assume she's arranged all of this so that she may be in control, what will happen to her?"

"By that time she will have achieved all that she wants, she actually arranged this marriage. In fact, she fought your engagement to Fortuno from the very beginning. She felt the Urbino line to be too weak to save our struggling coven.

My family, on the other hand, she felt a strong bond to. It was quite unfortunate the King's dying order was actually approved by the council. Though your mother petitioned them quite aggressively, they refused to budge. It was only then that our families were forced to come up with a new plan.

I am sorry for what you've had to suffer in the process, but I feel that once you've overcome your grief, you will find our engagement and subsequent marriage to be quite pleasing,"

Pem slapped his hand away angrily. This was ridiculous, she was a person with feelings, not some sort of bargaining chip!

"I will never overcome my grief enough to marry you!" she snapped angrily.

Salinar stepped closer and took her into his arms and pulled her roughly against his chest.

"Did I tell you that you basically have no choice in the matter? We are to be married, the council has endorsed it, you will abide by it," he barked.

"Take your hands off of me, I will never abide by it, no matter what the council says!"

Pem was struggling to get out of his arms, but he was too strong. Her struggling only made him press his body even tighter against hers and she could feel his growing erection pressing against her body. He breathed a deep sigh into her ear and trailed kisses down her neck, causing her to shiver.

He released her abruptly and she quickly inched back against the cool stone wall. Her breathing was fast and shallow, she was so overwhelmed by the feelings that were

rushing through her body right now, she wasn't sure what to think. She had almost felt desire for this man that she was certain she hated.

"Now I see why Fortuno was unable to wait another two years. I fear you've gotten to me as well," he breathed, flashing her a smoldering glance.

Pem was struggling to catch her breath, it was crazy, how could her body possibly want this man, when she obviously hated him with every fiber of her being?

"You must leave," she snapped, though her voice was shaky and unsure.

"Yes, I must. Lest I do something that we both will regret," he whispered, taking a bold step toward her.

Pem tried to step away, but he took her into his arms again.

"I don't want you to touch me!"

"Your entire body is trembling my love. Not with fear, but with desire. It will be quite perfect when I finally take you, but alas, I must wait."

"You must be completely delusional if you think I will ever willingly let you into my bed!" snapped Pem, angrily.

This was completely insane, she didn't love this man, how could she ever possibly allow him to make love to her?

"I believe you will. You still have a great many weeks of solitary confinement ahead of you. By the time you're done, you'll be begging for me. If not, there's always chains."

"What?"

"Chains my darling. You see the council has not only condoned our marriage but there is a binding betrothal contract. You have your royal duty to conceive a child with your rightful husband, willfully or in chains. The choice is yours..."

Pem glared at him as all of this sunk in. She was a prisoner and there was no way out of this demented intrigue, as far as she could tell.

She was engaged to a man she did not love and bound by law to have a child by him. She had been imprisoned for what seemed an eternity. She had no clue as to how long she'd been there in solitary and how long a sentence she had left. She couldn't stop the tears from coming to her eyes, her life would never be her own.

"How much longer must I serve this solitary confinement?" she sobbed. The stress of everything was finally taking over her brain.

"Only till you submit to being my wife," he told her with a bit of a smug smile.

"So forever then..." breathed Pem, her voice resigned.

"Or your eighteenth birthday, whichever comes first."

R. J. HANRAHAN

CHAPTER TEN

Weeks passed and Pem languished in her chambers without the comfort of human contact. There were no diversions, there was virtually nothing for her to do but gaze out the window. No books, no human contact, just the view of the nearby town and rolling green hills to pass the hours.

The servants went in and out without speaking a word to her, it was very unnerving. She longed to have something to occupy her mind besides the troubling memories of her undoing.

She had no word on her child, she had never laid eyes on him and she had no real confirmation that she even had a son. Her labor had seemed like a nightmare that she had awoken from abruptly and had suddenly been without child.

It was early one evening and the door to her room opened and a young, shy woman servant came into the room bearing her goblet of blood upon a silver tray. The girl was dressed in the fine livery of a castle servant and her red hair was gathered up in a shining bun at the base of her neck. Pem had already decided, she was going to make this woman talk.

"Hello," said Pem, quickly placing her body between the woman and the door.

The woman curtsied deeply and gave her a regal smile.

"Dear lady, what is your name?"

The woman shook her head and gave her a humble smile.

"I am your Queen and I command that you speak to me," snapped Pem, hoping desperately to use her rank to force the woman to speak.

"Please your majesty, I am sorry. I have taken a vow of silence. On pain of death I am not permitted to speak to you," said the woman, her face was now so frightened, it looked as if she might pass out.

"As I said, I am your Queen, any vows you have taken in front of the council, are null and void in my command," snapped Pem. She was painfully aware that she was making this all up as she went along, but it sounded good.

"As you wish, your majesty," said the woman, her stricken face was only slightly relieved by Pem's last statement.

"Tell me, what news can you give me of my child?"

"The Prince is well your majesty, he was a year old last month. A strong and handsome boy he is. He looks very much like your majesty," breathed the woman, she was so nervous she was shaking.

"You have seen him?" breathed Pem, she almost broke down at the very thought of her Prince. The child was a year old and she had never seen him.

"Yes, your majesty. For a time I was second maid to the nanny. Alas, Ludmilla did not want me taking care of her grandchild. There is very out rift between our families. That being said, I was reassigned to other roles within the castle."

"So you know the Prince well?"

"Yes, your majesty."

"Can you tell me about him? What does he look like?"

"Your majesty, I am very fearful speaking with you. Ludmilla has great powers. If she were to find out that I spoke with you, I have no idea what she..."

"Please, I am a mother who has never even seen her son. I beg you dear lady, tell me, I must know," breathed Pem, her heart was breaking. She needed to know more about her son.

The woman hesitated and reluctantly cleared her throat. "He's beautiful your majesty. He has blue eyes and ringlets of gold hair. He is probably the most beautiful child I have ever seen."

"Does he have a name?"

"Yes your majesty, he is Alexander of Milan."

"Milan? But how, we are not married?"

"Please do not ask these questions of me your majesty. I am but a servant and not worthy of speaking of such things. I only know what I have heard and that is your betrothal to Salinar of Milan has been ruled to be legal and binding with the council. The Prince was given his name now, on the promise of your marriage so that he not be considered a bastard."

Pem shook her head grimly. It didn't seem like it now, but she guessed things could be worse, at least her child was considered the Prince proper and she was still alive, at least she had that to be thankful for.

"Thank you for speaking with me, I appreciate your honesty," said Pem.

"Thank you, your majesty, I can only hope I will not pay with my life for it," said the girl.

"They cannot punish you, if they do not know," said Pem.

"They know, said the woman, never assume they aren't watching, for they always are."

CHAPTER ELEVEN

Many weeks passed, servants came in and out of her chambers, but none would break their vows of silence, even when Pem commanded them. The beautiful woman with the red hair never returned. Pem felt sick about it, but she was quite sure the woman was dead, and relatively sure it was her fault.

Early one evening the door to her room was flung open and there stood Salinar, his eyes raking over her arrogantly.

Her maids had dressed her in a flowing red silk dress with a deep square neckline and a fitted bodice that drew attention to her tiny waist and barely concealed her breasts. Her hair had been curled by her servants and piled loosely upon her head in an elegant mass.

Salinar gave her a curt bow from the doorway and crossed the room to her, unable to conceal his smile of adoration, she looked completely gorgeous, and she was all his.

"It is good to see you my Queen. You look quite lovely, it's as if you knew your future husband would pay you a visit today."

"Thank you for the compliment, even though I have no reason to dress up, curl my hair or even drag myself out of bed. I merely exist in this room. My beauty has more to do with the creativity of my servants than my own free will. I am dressed as I am simply because my servants made me so," said Pem, her voice was weak and resigned. She had been in solitary confinement for so long, she could barely stand it a moment longer. She wasn't sure why Salinar was here, but if this was to be her wedding day, she was almost happy for it.

"So I am guessing her majesty is tiring of her solitary confinement?"

"I imagine it is quite obvious, since even your presence here in my room seems to cheer me."

"I regret to inform you that as of today, you still have another six months to endure."

"Six months!" cried Pem, completely exasperated. How could she endure another six months of this torture? She needed something to divert her mind, she was about to go mad!

"I'm afraid so."

"Please, is there nothing that can be done?"

"Perhaps I could put in a good word with the council."

"Could you, please?" said Pem, way past the point of being too proud to beg.

"I most certainly could, but you must be willing to pay a bit of a price," said Salinar, a bit of an evil smile sneaking onto his lips.

"What price?" asked Pem, eyeing him suspiciously.

"Do not fear, it is not such a large price as you've paid in the past. But I must warn you, gaining such freedom does come at a bit of a premium."

Pem sighed, at this point she would agree to almost anything to be able to leave this room and possibly even see her son.

"You win, name your price, I can stand this no more."

"I have come to court you as my future wife. All I ask from you is that you be receptive to my...how shall I say it, demands."

"May I ask what are these...demands?" seethed Pem. She still loved Fortuno, but it was obvious that no matter what, she would end up married to this man. She was realizing she would be afforded many freedoms if she would only go along with it.

"Firstly, a kiss," he said, taking another bold step toward her.

Pem tried not to frown, it was only a kiss, she could at least give him that. He took her into his arms and gently took her lips in a soft kiss, Pem didn't resist him, but she didn't exactly participate either.

Unfortunately, Salinar was not about to let her remain uninvolved. His tongue touched her lips, urging them to part. As soon as Pem allowed his tongue into her mouth, the kiss grew deeper and more passionate. Salinar's arms tightened around her and in a matter of moments she was returning the passionate kiss.

Salinar pulled away abruptly, and Pem nearly fell over. She hadn't expected to be consumed by his kiss and she hadn't expected it to be over so quickly. Her eyes were averted in embarrassment, she couldn't look him in the eye, her chest was heaving with desire. Pem could feel her face turning a deep shade of crimson over the fact that his kiss had awakened something inside her that she thought was completely gone.

Salinar was walking slowly toward the door. He finally turned and looked her over casually.

"I'm sorry my Lady, I had to stop. Six months is a very long time to wait. I really didn't expect that you would respond to me like that, I thought that you would fight me."

"I am broken, the fight is gone," whispered Pem.

Pem looked down at the floor, unable to meet his gaze. She felt horrible for yielding to him so readily, but she was so desperate for human contact, she couldn't help herself.

"I am quite pleased you have finally come to your senses, I will have you moved to a regular room in the castle immediately. We will have a private dinner together tonight."

Pem couldn't speak, she merely nodded at him.

"Good evening my Queen," he told her, and he left the room.

Later that evening, she was moved to a larger, more beautiful room in the castle. There were books and cards, and servants that actually spoke to her. Compared to her previous lodgings it was as if she had died and gone to heaven. She wished she could see her son, but the servants all told her it was impossible. She had been granted access to most of the castle now, but the nursery remained off limits.

As the dinner hour approached, her servants dressed her in royal blue velvet and her golden hair was brushed till it shined and was twisted into an elegant chignon. A footman escorted her to the dinning room where an elaborate candelabra illuminated the large table which was set for two.

Salinar took her arm and escorted her to the table seating her in the chair to his left. The servants brought them their goblets and left them alone in the large and echoing dining room.

"Are you enjoying your newfound freedom my Queen?" asked Salinar, toasting her with his goblet.

"Yes, it is quite refreshing to be able to walk about the castle and not be confined to one room with nothing to amuse me but my views of the countryside."

"Now what amuses her majesty?"

"I may actually speak to my servants without fear of them being cruelly slaughtered, I have books and cards. It may not seem like much, but I am thankful."

"As am I. I have been waiting so very long for her majesty to be receptive of my courtship."

"What makes you certain that I am receptive now?" asked Pem.

"When I kissed you, you wanted me. I could feel your heart was pounding with desire. Soon, you will want me as much as I want you."

"I seriously doubt that," snapped Pem, rolling her eyes.

She took a deep breath, he was glaring at her. She knew she best not piss him off. He had given her a few freedoms, she had no doubt he could take them away. She knew she couldn't go back to solitary, she would lose her mind!

"Do not test me, your majesty. I have complete control over you for the next six months. It is best you not say something you might later regret."

Pem took a slow deep breath. Salinar was in complete control and she could barely stand it. She had always been a strong person, it was hard to be put in a position where you were so submissive.

"I'm very sorry, it's just that..."

"My Lord, you will call me my Lord. I am your Lord and master and you will show me the respect I deserve, do you understand, your Majesty?"

Pem almost shuddered, his voice was dripping with arrogance. She took a deep breath and nodded in resignation.

"Yes, my Lord."

"Thank you, your Majesty. Your obedience will be rewarded, if you continue to behave favorably. What can I do, that would please your Majesty?"

"I want to see my son," breathed Pem, her face was hopeful.

"That is a very big request, one that I cannot bequeath on my own. Such a request would have to go through the council and Ludmilla, of course," said Salinar, regarding her thoughtfully.

"Of course," said Pem, frowning.

"And it would come at a price..."

"I have no doubt it would," sighed Pem, resisting the urge to roll her eyes.

"If you will come with me to my chambers this evening we can discuss it further," he said, flashing her a smile.

Pem tried not to frown, she had a bit of an idea of what type of discussion they would have.

CHAPTER TWELVE

Pem returned to her chambers and plopped down numbly in a chair. Salinar made her nervous, but what could she do? She was nothing but a pawn in this demented game of chess. She barely even noticed when her maid arrived in the room and began fussing over her hair. She was not looking forward to being alone in Salinar's chambers with him, but if it afforded her a chance to see her son, then perhaps it would be worth it.

"Be very careful tonight, your Majesty," said the maid, speaking in low, hushed tones.

"I am spending the evening with my fiancee, why do you say such a thing, dear lady?" asked Pem, playing the part of the dumb child. She hoped that her maid would open up to her on her true thoughts of the Duke of Milan.

"It's just that the line of Milan was once the most ruthless and powerful bloodline in our coven..."

"Go on," said Pem, she knew nothing about the coven at all. How could she ever be expected to be Queen, when she was completely ignorant of the coven and it's long history.

"I am very sorry your majesty, I fear I've said too much already," said the woman, backing away slowly.

"Please, I need to know what I'm getting myself into," cried Pem.

"I'm sorry your Majesty, I cannot," the woman promptly headed to the door and fled the room, leaving Pem feeling anxious and overwhelmed.

Pem took a final look in the mirror and let herself out into the torchlit corridor. She knew the way to Salinar's chambers without being told. She also knew why she was going there.

Salinar had leverage right now, he was going to take advantage of it. She wanted desperately to see her son, he knew she would do whatever he asked of her.

Pem reached the door of Salinar's chambers and knocked.

"Come in my darling." he called.

Pem opened the door of his candlelit chamber. It was roughly the same size as hers, though it felt more masculine. As she entered she found the room had a slightly musky scent that she actually found a bit intriguing.

"I find it rather charming that this evening you are actually coming to me," said Salinar, smiling at her.

She nodded at him and gave him a slight shrug. What could she say? He had the advantage, she had to give him that.

"So what would you like to do, now that we are alone?" he asked, flashing her a slightly evil smile.

"Do you wish to play cards, my Lord?" asked Pem, trying to conceal the sly smile that automatically came to her lips.

"No, guess again my dear Lady."

"I have an inkling of what you have in mind, but I must warn you, the last man who did what you wish to do, was burned to death for doing so. I am just seventeen."

"I have had such a deed in mind for quite some time, but I shall wait a bit more, so not to anger the council. Though I must admit it will be hard to wait these last few months for

what I truly desire above all, I will inform you that there are other things you could do for me, that will keep me satisfied in the meantime," said Salinar, his eyes could not disguise the lust he was feeling.

"And if I do these things, you will allow me to see my son?"

"If you do them well," he said, flashing her an evil smile.

"I shall do whatever you ask, though I cannot guarantee that I will do it well."

"Whatever you do, I have no doubt it will make me happy."

Salinar took a cautious step toward his future bride. She was a rebellious one, but he was in complete control for the moment. She wanted to see her son, he could grant her such a wish, but only if she satisfied his rapidly growing desire. He wanted to take her right then and there, but he couldn't for he would suffer the same fate Fortuno had.

He had never met a woman who was so beautiful, yet so unbelievably headstrong as Pem. Their marriage would ensure that the coven's power would fall back to the line of Milan, though his upcoming marriage meant so much more to him. He would become the legal father to the future King and any children he had with Pem would be next in line to the throne.

Ludmilla had come to him after Fortuno had impregnated her daughter and married her in a lame attempt to patch things up with the council. Ludmilla had not been happy about the match in the first place, she was loyal to the line of Milan.

Salinar sometimes wondered if Ludmilla had somehow caused Fortuno to slip up. Ludmilla was powerful, that was the main reason he hoped to remain in her good graces. He would not make love to her daughter before legally

allowed. But that didn't keep him from getting his sexual gratification in other ways.

Pem was almost shaking as Salinar came to her and put his arms around her, she had no idea what he wanted from her, she only knew she must not let him make love to her. She'd end up with quite the reputation if she had two future husbands killed off.

Salinar put his arms around her and began kissing her. Her lips parted easily to allow his tongue into her mouth. Salinar couldn't help but chalk that up as a bit of a victory. He was hoping she would willingly submit to whatever he wanted. She wanted to see her baby and she was going to do whatever it took to accomplish that goal. By law they couldn't go all the way, but there was no law to keep them from satisfying their desires in other ways.

Salinar couldn't help his hands from roaming, his future wife had a beautiful body and he couldn't keep his hands off of it. His hands slid down her back, tracing her hips and grasping her firm buttocks.

Pem let out a slight moan of approval and pressed her body tighter against his. He could feel his heart racing and the rest of his body responding as well. He cupped her breast with his right hand, sliding it out of her low cut bodice and rubbing his fingers across the nipple until it was taunt and hard.

Pem was breathing heavily as he took her nipple into his mouth, sucking hard, causing her to gasp with pleasure. Her body was writhing in response to his touch. He was so aroused now, he felt as if his erection might break through the fabric of his pants. He had both of her breasts in his hands and was dividing his attention between both nipples, causing Pem to writhe uncontrollably. He planned to bring her to orgasm and hopefully she would willingly repay the favor.

He was dying to put his hand between her legs, just to find out how turned on she was. He bit her nipple playfully and began pulling back the many layers of fabric between him and his intended target.

"No, we can't," breathed Pem, her hand clamped down on his wrist.

"Trust me my love, I won't ruin everything for us," he breathed, slowly sliding his hand up her thigh.

Pem gasped as he parted her legs to explore the warm wetness he found there. Pem squirmed, unable to believe the sensations he was awakening in her. His fingers began to explore her and were soon plunging inside of her, reveling in her wetness, working feverishly, urging her to let herself go.

As his fingers skillfully brought her to an orgasm, Pem cried out, her body writhing uncontrollably. Just when she thought she had died and went to heaven, he lifted her skirt a bit more, shifted his body lower, and buried his face between her legs.

Pem wasn't sure what was happening until she felt him spreading her apart and flickering his tongue inside her. Pem couldn't help but cry out, it felt so good. Within moments she was moaning and writhing uncontrollably, she had never felt anything like that in her entire life!

In moments, she felt a wave of ecstasy, it was almost as if her entire body were turning inside out. She was literally shouting out as he brought her to another orgasm that left her gasping to breathe.

"Did you like it my darling?" he asked her as he snuggled next to her, rubbing his thumb across her rock hard nipple and kissing her.

"Yes," she breathed, barely able to catch her breath.

"Do you know now, what you can do for me?" he asked.

Pem nodded. She'd heard of oral sex, but she had no experience. After her own orgasm, she had no confidence that she could have that kind of effect on Salinar. He obviously knew what he was doing, she on the other hand, had no clue.

"I will try my Lord, I have never done such a thing," said Pem, trying to hide her embarrassment, with the situation.

"Really?" Salinar seemed to be astonished that she had never performed oral sex. "Fortuno must have been stupider than I had thought. You could have completely satisfied his lust without losing your virginity."

Pem sighed, she knew that the entire point of the spell, or whatever the hell it had been was for her to lose her virginity.

"Tell me what to do," said Pem, she was determined to please him, she wanted to see her son so badly. Besides, after what he had just done to her, if she did half as well, she guessed he would be happy.

"Since you've never done this before, you'll want to start slow, hold it, lick it like a popsicle at first, later when you feel more comfortable you can put the entire thing in your mouth...till I cum.

Pem shifted her body so she could pleasure him. His member was already large and engorged, she took it into her hands and touched her tongue to it. He moaned in approval,

she licked some more and it felt as if it was growing even harder.

Pem was encouraged, Salinar's entire body had stiffened and his face was contorted in ecstasy. Pem darted her tongue across the tip and slowly took the thick head into her mouth. Salinar gasped and pushed it a bit deeper into her mouth, she seemed to be doing well enough, at least she wasn't gagging.

His body was soon bucking with a rhythm, pushing his swollen cock into her mouth a bit further with every stroke. Soon Pem had the entire thing in her mouth. It wasn't horrible like she had thought, she was watching his face as she took him deeper and deeper into her mouth and throat. He was moaning loudly and she almost giggled when she thought about all the noise she'd made when he had brought her to her orgasm.

His hips were moving faster now, bucking in a quickening rhythm that told her that his climax was coming soon. In moments she felt his cock spasm and he let out a loud shout as he filled the back of her throat with cum.

Just watching the pleasure on his face was completely amazing thought Pem, as she sucked up every last bit of his cum. He had fallen back into the pillows and was panting gratefully.

In a few moments he gathered Pem into his arms and kissed her.

"You have definitely earned yourself a visit with the Prince. Sleep with me now my darling and when we awake you shall see your young Prince," said Salinar, kissing her on the forehead and promptly falling asleep.

CHAPTER THIRTEEN

Pem awoke to the sun streaming in through the leaded glass windows of Salinar's chamber. They were tangled in the sheets and she was still wrapped in his strong arms. She almost giggled with embarrassment, if his manservant came in, he'd think they had already consummated their marriage.

She started to get up, but Salinar's arms tightened around her.

"Where are you going?" he breathed sleepily.

"Back to my room, before someone thinks..."

"My darling, we are vampires, most of us are capable of feeling the feelings of others. Even if the servants see us in bed together they will know. We are sharing our love for one another, but we have not done anything illegal."

"Are you saying they will know what we've done?" cried Pem, suddenly embarrassed.

"It is nothing to be ashamed of my darling. We all have urges. It is perfectly natural that we satisfy those urges.

Blazes, I was so excited to have you here, I forgot to close the drapes. My corneas will be burned to a crisp!" he declared, jumping from the bed to close the drapes.

Pem sighed, this new life of hers was very strange. She wasn't sure she would ever fit into this new world, but what could she do now? She was one of them, forever...

She was anxious to go and meet her son, but it seemed as if the only thing Salinar was anxious to do was a repeat performance of last night. He was kissing and caressing her,

his hand was sneaking down between her legs once again. After he had given her several intense orgasms, she returned the favor to him. It was satisfying, but the more she had his enormous cock in her mouth, the more the couldn't wait to feel him cum inside her. It was going to feel completely amazing to have him slide into her when she was all wet and worked up.

"Will we be doing this often?" asked Pem, rolling over and brushing his hair out of his face?

"As often as we can get away with," he said, flashing her a smile.

"What if we can't stop?" asked Pem.

"We will, because we must. It won't be long now." he told her, kissing her on the forehead.

"But what if my mother..."

"No, this time your mother is on our side. I'm aware that some people are under the impression that she had something to do with Fortuno's death, but that's not true. That is nothing but a cruel rumor."

"But that's just it, it's not. She did something to me. It was a spell or something. It was all my fault. I seduced him. I made Fortuno make love to me," cried Pem, she was suddenly frightened that the same thing would happen to them.

"Believe me, I know your mother. She was against your marriage to Fortuno from the very beginning. She wants us to be married, to bring the power back to the Milan line. Whatever spell that has been cast over me, it's been cast by you. I cannot seem to get enough of you."

"Me either, it's why I'm worried, maybe we should try to stay apart, until I'm eighteen." said Pem, obviously nervous about the entire situation.

"I wish I could, but I cannot. I love you, I want you more than I've wanted anything. I cannot wait until out wedding day."

Pem smiled and snuggled into his arms, she believed that he loved her, though she wasn't quite sure she could say the same thing. She desired him, she knew that much, but love...that was a different story. She wished she knew more about the coven and why her mother thought a match with the Milan line was so important. She would have to do her research.

Her maid came to the chambers to get her dressed. She felt embarrassed that she had spent the night with Salinar, but her maid didn't seem to be a bit shocked with the situation.

Salinar escorted her into the dining room and sat her at the table. In a matter of moments trumpets blared out the arrival of the Prince. His nanny carried him through the velvet draped doorway and Pem stood up immediately.

The maid carried him over to her and let Pem take him from her arms. Pem could feel tears coming to her eyes as she held her son in her arms for the very first time.

He was just as beautiful as she'd been told. He was pudgy cheeked with bright blue eyes and ringlets of golden blonde hair.

"My baby," sighed Pem, as she hugged the child against her chest.

"Mama," said the boy, snuggling into the crock between her neck and shoulder.

Both Salinar and the maid had tears in their eyes as mother and baby were united for the first time. Pem was so entranced by the child, she had completely forgotten how ravenously hungry she was.

When the maid finally announced that she must take him back to the nursery, Pem regretfully released him and returned to the table. When she saw the goblet in front of her she drained the entire goblet in one long gulp.

"My darling I must say, your hunger for blood almost eclipses your hunger for me," said Salinar, flashing her an appreciative grin.

"Almost," said Pem.

CHAPTER FOURTEEN

With her eighteenth birthday just two months away Pem was finally starting to a bit feel better about her situation. The wedding preparations were coming along and she got to spend time each day with Alexander, even though she had no control over the child's life as of yet.

Having free access to the entire castle was nice, she loved exploring the castle, especially it's expansive library.

She had found several books describing in detail, the colorful history of their coven. The history was mired by wars with other covens and even senseless feuds between the families within. Pem was distressed to confirm, what she had already suspected about her presence at the castle. She was merely a pawn in a longstanding game of political chess. Each family would make it's move and watch anxiously to see what the opposing family would do about. It all seemed rather childish to Pem.

It seems the power hungry Milan branch of the coven had ruled their dynasty for quite some time. Pem's own mother Ludmilla, was princess of the Venezia line, a very old, royal bloodline, who boasted it's share of great Kings and Queens, but at some point their power had fallen to the Urbino line. In an effort to bring his bloodline back to the throne, Ludmilla's father had her betrothed to King Vitale of the Urbino line. The King was not the greatest of rulers, but he was a great fan of Ludmilla's stunning beauty.

Ludmilla, on the other hand, found the King's personality "tiresome" and she described him as mousy looking and not handsome at all. Ludmilla was quite smart and power hungry, which caused her father to assume that becoming Queen Consort to the coven would be enough for Ludmilla to give up her life forever to a man she had no attraction to.

Ludmilla's distaste for the King was evident to all who knew her, fueling fears that she would dishonor her betrothal. As rumors flew throughout the kingdom, the king began to make plans to keep the power of the coven with the Urbino line.

His betrothal to Ludmilla would unite his family with the line of Venezia. He knew a marriage linking a Venezia and a Urbino would breed a powerful King, but he feared that Ludmilla would betray him somehow and the Urbino family would lose control of the coven.

To protect his own family's line, he wrote out a humiliation clause to be added to his betrothal. If Ludmilla were to break her marriage contract, the power of the coven would return to the line of Urbino and his only cousin, Fortuno.

As it turned out, Ludmilla did indeed scorn the King, the very night of their wedding. With that act, and the King's subsequent death, the humiliation clause of the contract went into effect. Ludmilla's first born daughter would be betrothed to Fortuno, the King's only cousin, thus ensuring the line of succession fall back to the Urbinos.

Ludmilla, not having read the marriage contract fully, was completely mortified. She had no desire to have the lines of succession back in the hands of the Urbinos. She left the coven in anger with a new plan. She thought that by marrying and producing children with a mortal man, she could anger the council enough that her future offspring would be free from the politics of the coven and not eligible to be in line for the crown.

Unfortunately, what was promised, was promised. The will of the King could not be undone. The Urbino line was pleased with the arrangements, even though Fortuno's betrothed would be a half breed. They felt that with the royal

blood of Ludmilla's offspring in their line, their power would be unstoppable.

And so came the betrothal between Fortuno and Pemberthy. Unable to convince the council that the late King's forced betrothal of her daughter was an act of vengeance, Ludmilla became obsessed with finding another way of stopping the marriage between Fortuno and Pem.

Pem wanted to hate her mother for what she had done, but she still had no idea of how deeply these family lines ran within the coven. She had no desire to begin her reign as Queen in the midst of an ancient family feud. Perhaps her marriage to Salinar would patch things up a bit within the coven.

At dinner, she talked to Salinar about what she had read. He was frowning in disapproval. "I wish you would just leave the politics to me. Your job is to be faithful to me and bear me heirs to the throne, do you understand?"

"I may be young, but I'm not stupid. I just want to understand how things got to this point. I want to understand how my mother could have betrayed her own daughter like that."

"You? You aren't the one betrothed to a bloody half breed who's already bore a bastard child! Think how I feel," cried Salinar, angrily.

Pem glared at him soberly, she'd never thought of it that way. His harsh words had shook her up, he had told her that he loved her, and she had believed him. Now she was beginning to believe it wasn't true. It seemed he was just doing what was required to rule their coven. Apparently, what he needed to do was honor his betrothal to a filthy half breed, slut who would restore power to his family's line.

"I'm glad I finally know the truth about how you feel. I was under the impression that you actually loved me," snapped Pem.

"I do love you darling. Do not be angry with me, I confess, I wasn't keen on the idea of our marriage at first. My misgivings had nothing to do with you personally, but I was worried about taking on the Prince, you know, him not being my blood..."

"And what shall happen to Alexander? He is of Urbino blood, not a Milan. Will he be killed off in favor of our children? I don't think I could allow that to happen."

"Don't worry about the boy. The Venezia family has their own strengths. He will be sworn in to council as a Venezia and officially given my name when we marry. Most of the coven will have no qualms about his legitimacy."

"Most of the coven," said Pem, rolling her eyes.

"It cannot be helped, there are some that will never accept him. If your mother had been more clever, she might have thought up a better plan to rid you of your unwanted fiancee."

Pem frowned. "Do you blame me?"

"For the child? Certainly not. I realize your mother is quite powerful, one of the most powerful and gifted members of our coven. I have no doubt that she put some sort of a spell on you, add to the that the fact that you have a large sexual appetite in the first place and I can see no help for it," said Salinar, shaking his head dismissively.

"Thank you," said Pem.

"As I said, keep out of the politics and things will go well for you, in two months you shall be my wife."

"But if I am to be Queen, don't you think I should educate myself about the coven and it's history?"

"Queen in title only, my love. Like I said, I will handle the politics, your duty is to support me."

"Support you? I am the sole reason you are going to be the King consort in the first place," cried Pem.

"I am also the sole reason you are even still alive. I agreed to marry you to keep you from the same fate as your traitorous husband. The only reason the council agreed to this marriage, is that they couldn't pass up a chance to keep the Venezia bloodline in the coven monarchy. Even as a half breed, I have no doubt your family's greatest strengths will be passed down to our children. Alexander may be the one destined to be King, but our children will also possess a great deal of power," said Salinar, assessing her cooly.

Pem had narrowed her eyes at him. He obviously thought she was stupid, if he thought that she was going to sit back and let him handle all the politics, he was in for a rude awakening. She refused to be nothing but a brood mare for the coven.

She wanted to say more, but she kept her mouth clamped shut. Perhaps he was right about the council. They hadn't tried her for treason, even though she was just as guilty as Fortuno had been. She had dishonored the monarchy by bearing a bastard son. She was not happy about her past, but at least she still had a future. When she wed Salinar two months from now she would be Queen consort, whether he liked it, or not. If he was using her to get to the throne, perhaps she could use him just as easily.

He had now given her back her freedom, maybe once she had given him a child he would relent and let her share the responsibilities of the kingdom.

Salinar stood up and gave her a kiss on the cheek. "I'm going to retire to my chambers, I will see you tomorrow."

"You are retiring alone?" she asked, flashing him a sly smile.

"We have but two months to wait, I don't want to tempt fate. You can be good for two months, can't you?"

"I shall try my Lord," said Pem.

Pem returned to her own chambers, pondering the conversation they'd had tonight. He was using her, that much was obvious, but he was absolutely right, if he had not agreed to the betrothal, she would have probably burned along with Fortuno, royal bloodline or not.

She was infinitely glad that she was no longer in solitary confinement. It seemed odd that he was retiring alone tonight. It seemed as if all of a sudden, he had no urge to play the sexual games they had engaged in over the last several months. Perhaps he had tired of shooting his load into her mouth, between her breasts or onto her stomach as they pushed each other to their limits every night, perhaps it was becoming too much for him to endure.

Pem sighed with regret, she loved it when he brought her to orgasm, she wondered how could she live without it for the next two months.

She felt lonely by herself in her chambers every night and morning, sometimes she would touch herself, the way he touched her, hoping she could bring the same feeling to herself. It was exciting, but not the same. Salinar was so

strong and forceful, it only took moments for him to have her writhing uncontrollably.

One evening, her maid walked in and caught her as she was touching herself. The poor, shocked woman tried to bow out of the room gracefully, but Pem called to her.

"Wait," called Pem, clutching the sheets around her naked body.

"Your majesty, I am sorry, I didn't realize..." said the woman, bowing to her, completely red faced.

"No, I'm sorry, it's just that Salinar used to spend the night with me. Don't get me wrong, we didn't do it, but I do miss his touch. Do you think men do that? Touch themselves?

"I am sure they do it a lot more than they're willing to admit."

Pem smiled, now she didn't feel like so much of a freak. She wondered if Salinar was touching himself now, thinking about her.

"His Lordship is lucky. I doubt he has the need to touch himself. The men of the royal court have their pick of the courtesans," said the lady.

"Courtesans?" cried Pem.

"You know, women who service them sexually. I guess in the society you come from they call them prostitutes," said the woman, blushing again.

"I know what they are, are you saying that Salinar has one?"

"Several, I have heard," said the woman.

"Salinar has **several** courtesans!" cried Pem, completely horrified.

"Do not be upset! It is not abnormal here in our kingdom, especially for royalty. For men it is more about the act, than the emotion. Even more so in our vampire race, the men want sex for the release it brings them. I know for mortals it is more about emotion, but not so much for us."

"Oh my God! He tells me I must be faithful to him, yet he sees no harm in having sex with sluts!" cried Pem, her face was red with anger.

"I am very sorry my lady, it's really not fair for us, being women, it is the curse of childbearing."

"What?"

"Being a woman, your body has been designed to bear vampire babies. Unlike a mortal, pregnancy is not a chance for us, it is a certainty. If the seed is delivered to your womb you will become pregnant, it is why our council is so serious about marriage."

Pem's eyes were wide with understanding, it was no wonder her one thoughtless tryst had ended in pregnancy, it was no wonder Fortuno had been so frantic to get back to the castle and get married.

"In fact, your lady, the beautiful one with red hair was pregnant with Salinar's child. The council had her burned, before word got out."

"Oh my God!" cried Pem. "How many bastard babies does he have?"

"Well none, as far as I know. Courtesans don't get pregnant very often. They have trained themselves to give pleasure,

not receive it. They have found they can prevent pregnancy, if they don't have an orgasm.

They have found that it is the rhythmic spasm of a woman's own orgasm that pulls the man's seed into the womb where conception happens almost immediately.

Many try to please their men in other ways, though it isn't long though before the man demands intercourse. Many of these woman have programed their minds in such a way that they can have sex with a man without having an orgasm at all.

Unfortunately, sometimes they slip up, they get carried away. Of course, then they find themselves pregnant with a baby that their master will never, ever acknowledge. The council does away with them before their pregnancy is evident to the others."

Pem was throwing on her robe and pacing the room nervously.

"This is completely unacceptable. What can I do?" she cried, pacing nervously.

"I'm afraid that there is nothing you can do your Majesty, it's just how things are."

"And after we are married, will he still use the services of these courtesans then?"

"Most likely your Majesty. Men tend to get bored with just one woman, they...."

"That bastard!" cried Pem, rushing to the door and flinging it open. She stepped out into the torchlit hall, determined to have it out with her future husband.

She reached his room and flung the door open without knocking, she was only mildly surprised to find a beautiful woman on top of him, her naked breasts bouncing each time he thrust into her.

The shocked couple immediately stopped what they were doing and the woman rolled out of the bed and slunk away quickly, wrapped in a sheet. Salinar lay there staring at her as he struggled to catch his breath.

"What brings you to my chambers?" he asked, almost half joking.

"Are you fucking insane?" cried Pem, her angry voice echoed through the large room.

"Are you angry my love?" he asked, finally.

"Of course I'm angry! I walk into your room and you're fucking another woman, how the hell do expect me to feel?"

"I'm sure you've heard this before, but all men have needs..."

"So you just hop into bed with whatever slut you can find!"

"Darling, I am trying to make this work. Trying to respect the laws of our coven and wait till you are eighteen. Soon we will marry and I will be able to make love to you."

"No, I will not marry you."

"You have no choice my dear, the marriage contract is binding."

"And these women that you have sex with, will it end when we are married?"

"Of course, for a while. Though soon I will grow bored and want something new. It is the curse of being a man, we cannot help it."

"I will go to the council, they will never make me marry a man who is going to be unfaithful to me." cried Pem.

"Don't be ridiculous, who do you think finds me my sluts? These courtesans are arranged for me by the men of the court and the council. Do not worry my darling, these woman are trained to resist their own sexual satisfaction, they will not get pregnant. They know if they do, they will be burned. It's as simple as that."

"I don't want any part of this," cried Pem

"It is too late my darling. We are betrothed, we will be married and you will bear my children."

"Not if I never let you make love to me," cried Pem.

"It is your duty, I already told you Pem, you will give me children either with chains or without. It's your choice."

CHAPTER FIFTEEN

Pem sat at the dressing table as her maid finished   putting her hair up. The maid was draping strands of pearls in her thick, blonde curls and placing her sixteen foot long veil upon her head. Pem let out a impotent sigh, she didn't want to go through with this marriage, but she'd already exhausted every resource she thought might be able to stop this wedding.

Today she would marry Salinar, though she was not happy about it. She could not change the will of the council, it refused to break the betrothal contract.

Pem was worried about Alexander, he was not Salinar's blood, though as part of the betrothal contract, he'd already given him his family name. Alexander was now a Milan, and she would be as well. Pem was trapped, Salinar had control of her from the very beginning and because she loved her son, he would now have control of her forever.

The wedding had the entire coven in a frenzy, but it was not surprising, how often does a royal wedding happen? Not very often in vampire covens. Except in extenuating circumstances, vampires live forever.

A vampire can burn of course, if convicted of certain crimes. They can, lose the will to live and die, possibly of a broken heart. For the most part, marriage was forever. Pem was not happy to be enslaved forever to a man who desired to control her and her son, who was destined to be King.

If something were to happen to Alexander, the King and Queen consort, who would be herself and Salinar, would take the throne. Pem couldn't help but fear for her son's life, Alexander was an Urbino, if the Milans wanted him dead, how could she possibly protect him?

Pem could feel her whole body shaking as her maids fussed about her, putting the finishing touches on her hair and veil. She hoped that her anxiety weakened legs would get her all the way down the long aisle of the massive stone chapel.

On an attendant's cue she walked slowly down the candle lit aisle alone, in the coven tradition. She could see Salinar at the altar with the rest of the wedding party. He was dressed in gold silk that glowed in the candlelight. Her own white silk gown was trimmed in gold and shimmered like a beacon of light as she approached the elaborate altar.

As she reached the front of the church Salinar stepped forward to take her hand. He led her slowly toward the clergy, bowing forward in an effort to see her face through the veil in the flickering candle light.

"No shenanigans tonight. I'm very serious my love, I know you've been angry with me, but no matter how you feel, do not make a scene," he whispered.

Pem thought about Alexander and how much she loved him. She could never do anything that would endanger his life.

"Don't be daft darling, I gave my word...I will marry you."

He gave her a smile, but Pem felt smug. She had promised to marry him, but she had not promised to consummate their marriage. He had courtesans, what did he need her for? To have a child? She already had a child, that was enough for her.

The wedding ceremony was beautiful and the reception that followed had music, dancing and goblet after goblet of blood.

Just after midnight Salinar took her by the hand and told her it was time to go. The party was still going strong and she

hated to leave, but she followed him anyway. When they reached the upstairs hallway she turned to head to her room.

"Oh no you don't," said Salinar, turning her and pointing her toward his chambers.

"There's no need for me to go to your chambers with you, I promised to marry you, that is all. If you want to fuck someone, you must fuck one of your courtesans, that is what you've been doing the past two months anyway," she snapped angrily.

"Someone has acquired a smart mouth and a bit of an attitude over the past several months," seethed Salinar, his eyes raking over her angrily.

"Someone has had her eyes opened to the world that we live in and she doesn't care for it much."

"Well in this world you are my wife, part of a binding contact that must be honored."

"I have married you, I have fulfilled my part of the contract."

"I'm afraid not, our marriage is meant to be more than just our signatures on a piece of paper. As Queen consort you are bound by the expectation of heirs," snapped Salinar, growing more impatient with his new wife by the second.

"I also thought that our marriage was meant to be more than signatures on a piece of paper, until I caught you disrespecting me with some nameless whore you chose to fuck."

"I'm sure you realize my darling, all men have needs. For the vampire race, the needs are intensified, you cannot simply put it out of your mind. That bimbo meant nothing to me, it was purely physical."

"I don't care what she meant to you. I thought you loved me," spat Pem.

"I do love you. You are my wife Pem, and as my wife you will honor our marriage vows. Everyone is expecting us to consummate our marriage."

"I guess they'll all be a bit disappointed then, won't they?" Pem gave him a smug smile. If he thought she was going to sleep with him merely because he commanded her to, he was about to suffer a great disappointment.

Salinar merely grabbed her by the wrist and manhandled her roughly into his chambers.

"I'm guessing no one will be disappointed tonight," he seethed.

He jostled her roughly into the room, Pem was startled as she glanced slowly around the candlelit room. It looked much different from the last time she had been there, it had recently been outfitted with heavy iron chains which hung ominously from the ceiling.

Pem drew in a deep, shaky breath. She had thought his arrogant boast about placing her in chains had been an idle threat, but it was obvious now, he was completely serious. Obviously, didn't want to take any chances that she might put up a fight.

"So how's it going to be my wife, chains or no chains?"

Pem gave him a resentful glare and spun around to leave the room. That was when some strange, unknown force pulled her back into the room and immediately enslaved her in the chains that were hanging from the ceiling.

Salinar laughed heartily and gave her an amused smile.

"Nice try, but it's going to take a little bit more than walking away to deter me from my goal. I know you are new to our kingdom, but perhaps it's time for you to get to know the powers I possess."

"You would really force me to have sex with you?" snapped Pem, she was angry, she had no idea he would use force or chains, this was a nightmare!

"Force is such a nasty word, it reeks of rape, something I myself, would never condone. I would, on the other hand, encourage you to submit to what is expected of you. You see, according to coven law we have exactly twenty four hours to consummate our marriage. Should more time than that elapse, the council will send witnesses," said Salinar, flashing her a smug smile.

"Witnesses!" cried Pem completely horrified.

"Just in case you need a crowd to cheer you on," he told her, barely able to conceal his amusement with the situation.

"That is the most ridiculous thing I have ever heard in my entire life, you are lying!"

"I only wish that I were, but as you know, you are Royalty. In the old days the council always came to witness, you know, to make sure the marriage wasn't a complete sham."

"I have never heard of anything so ridiculous in my life!" cried Pem.

"Well, I regret to inform you that you're not in Kansas anymore, Dorothy."

"Take these chains off of me," demanded Pem. She was nearly ready to give in.

"I'm sorry my dear, you've already tried to leave once, as far as I'm concerned, your decision has already been made. You are a bit overdressed though. Salinar waved his arm and in a flash of light she was standing there naked, in front of him.

Pem was shivering in the candlelight, her wrists and ankles in irons. Salinar was ambling slowly around her, regarding her with amusement. He was obviously enjoying himself, controlling her, making her submit completely to him. Pem wished he would let her get into the bed, but it was obvious he wanted her humiliation to be complete since she had defied him.

"Well, are you going to do it or not?" cried Pem, he was beginning to piss her off.

"In good time my darling. Perhaps I want you to ponder your disobedience a bit longer. Remember, you promised to obey your Lord and Master."

"You will never be my Lord and Master. If you want to fuck me, just get it over with," snapped Pem.

"Maybe I want you to wait just a bit longer for the most perfect orgasm you have ever experienced."

"You may try my Lord, I will set my mind, like a courtesan and refuse to receive any pleasure from your lovemaking. Then we will not conceive a child and you will have wasted your time," said Pem.

"If I receive pleasure from our coupling, I guarantee I will not feel as if I've wasted my time. In any case, I am in control now. You have been a selfish young lady tonight. You

thought that you could satisfy the council by marrying me, but refusing to do your wifely duties. I hate to tell you, but that will never go over with me, or the council."

"Selfish perhaps, but you are nothing but a filthy pig!"

"I may be a filthy pig, but I've just married a dishonored slut with a bastard child. Neither of us is perfect, so get over it," raged Salinar.

"You knew exactly what I was, still, you chose to marry me."

"So we've both lain with others, it is of no consequence to me. I accepted your bastard child and gave him my family name, you will accept that I have laid with whores."

"I'm guessing Fortuno was one hundred times better lover than you'll ever be," snapped Pem, her voice raising in anger.

"Well, you're about to find out my darling."

Salinar was moving closer to her, he walked all around her slowly, like a wildcat stalking it's prey. It was making Pem shake even harder. She had angered him and he intended to make her humiliation complete. Finally, he came to her and stood there, just inches away.

"Salinar, take the irons off, you've made your point," sighed Pem. She was tired of his attempts to intimidate her.

"I have not even begun to make my point," seethed Salinar, placing one hand on each cheek and kissing her deeply. His hands slid down the sides of her neck, down to cup each breast and caress them. Then he slid his hands down between her legs, carefully spreading her apart, slowly dipping a finger in, then two.

"My darling wife, you are dripping wet, I find this odd since you said you didn't want me," his voice was silky with malice.

"Just do what you have to do and get it over with," snapped Pem.

"I will not have an eighteen year old child telling me what to do. If you are jealous of my whores you will do what they do and keep your smart mouth shut, unless of course, it has my cock in it," he snapped.

"How dare you speak to me like that," cried Pem.

"I believe I told you to keep your mouth shut," snapped Salinar.

He walked around until he was standing behind her, Pem was struggling to see what he was doing, but the chains didn't allow her much movement. She gasped as Salinar suddenly placed both his palms on her shoulders and bent her over as far as the irons on her wrists would allow. Salinar slid two fingers into her already wet slit. Pem was trying to be as emotionless as possible but a low moan escaped her lips.

"Uh, huh. I knew you wanted it. Here we go my darling,"said Salinar, sliding his cock in quickly, before she could resist him. He let out a groan of satisfaction as he slid himself into her, full length.

Pem grunted, he was so large, it was almost painful at first. Then he started moving inside her. She tried to keep her lips shut but the harder he thrusted inside her, the more the moans kept escaping her lips.

Salinar was getting more excited by the moment. His pace was increasing rapidly, Pem was restrained so she had no choice but to stand there as he rammed into her again and

again. Pem had already decided she would pretend she was a courtesan, if she set her mind to it, she wouldn't have an orgasm. No orgasm, no baby. That would make Salinar angry.

As the pace and intensity of his thrusting increased, Pem couldn't help it, she was so wet and he was so hard, and as he was entering her from behind his large cock was achieving maximum penetration. She had never experienced anything like this before. With each thrust she was crying out and she soon realized she was so close to an orgasm, there would be no holding back.

Salinar had doubled the pace of his thrusts, he was close now, but so was Pem. She had angered him, which made him feel he had to prove a point. The point was, if he wanted her to have an orgasm, she would have one, and she would be pregnant with his child.

He knew she was close, her breathing had disintegrated into mere gasps and he could hold back no longer. When he finally exploded inside her, she rewarded him with her own powerful orgasm. Pem let out a wail as her entire body was raked with spasms. Salinar couldn't help but smile as he felt her orgasm, it was like a bet won for him.

"You thought you could hold back didn't you?"

"You pig, shut up, you got what you wanted," snapped Pem.

"You make a better Queen than a courtesan," he laughed, as he slowly withdrew from her.

"With any luck, I'm not pregnant."

"I guarantee you are my love, I felt your spasms drawing my seed into your womb. Our child is growing within you as we speak."

"Splendid, what now?" groaned Pem.

"I will release you from the irons if you promise not to hit me,"said Salinar.

"What good would hitting you do if I am already pregnant?"

"Why are you so against having another child?" he asked, releasing the chains and turning her around so that he could look into her eyes.

"I'm not against having another child. I'm against having another child with you."

"You are the acting Queen, it is your duty to have heirs, and lots of them. I have given your bastard child my name and when he reaches the legal age he will be King. Please be happy for what you have. If it weren't for me, you'd have burned right beside Fortuno, with your baby still in your womb.

Pem shivered. She knew he was right. She could feel their recently conceived child burning inside her womb. She knew she was lucky, she was alive, her child was alive and destined to be King. It seemed that for now it was best to just go along with this senseless charade, what else could she do?

CHAPTER SIXTEEN

The sun was peeking through a large gap in the thick velvet draperies of her chamber, causing Pem to roll around restlessly in her bed for a few minutes. Finally, unable to stand the unpleasant sensation any longer, she got up and pulled the draperies together tightly, so there was barely any gap at all. The light had never really bothered her so much before, but it did now, for some reason.

Pem crawled back into bed and pulled the covers over her head, trying her hardest to fall back to sleep before her memories of the evening before came tumbling back, but it was too late, she was already ruing ever waking up at all.

She was now married to a man she could barely stand and if her intuition was right, she was already carrying his child, she had felt this burning in her womb before. The last time it had been a joyful sensation, this time though, not so much. She only hoped that since she'd done her duty and conceived a child with him, he would leave her alone. She'd heard he had access to numerous courtesans, why would he come to her?

She finally fell back to sleep and when she awoke the room had been cooled by just a kiss of an evening breeze and the sun was sinking below the horizon in the west.

Pem sat up and stretched lazily, feeling deliciously rested. There was a rap on the door that startled her.

"What!" she screeched, assuming it was Salinar. She'd had her fill of him and at this point she wouldn't care if he never showed his face around her again.

The door opened and a maiden servant carrying a tray with a goblet of blood walked in. She poor maid was quite nervous but she managed a shaky curtsy.

"Sorry, I didn't mean to snap at you, I thought you were Salinar," said Pem, giving the maid a sheepish smile and taking the goblet from the tray.

The girl blushed at the mention of Salinar's name, curtsied again and quickly left the room. Pem sighed and shook her head in disgust. Why had the very mention of Salinar's name caused that young girl to blush and scurry away like that? Was this young maid one of his many concubines? Of course, why wouldn't that young, beautiful thing be one of Salinar's sluts?

If Pem hadn't been so ravenously hungry, she would have taken the goblet full of blood and flung it against the wall. Unfortunately, she was pregnant and her body needed every drop of that blood to nourish her quickly growing fetus.

How could Salinar's infidelity make her so angry when she didn't even love him? She just wanted to claw his eyes out, but that was silly, she would get her revenge with Salinar in other ways.

A short time later the door to her chambers was flung open and Salinar was standing there in the doorway grinning at her.

"Have you ever heard of knocking?" asked Pem, her voice could not conceal the sarcasm that was sneaking into it.

"So you could refuse me entry? I do not think so. How do you feel tonight my beautiful wife?"

"What do you care?"

"I care a great deal about my wife and the tiny daughter she is now carrying in her womb," said Salinar, walking a bit closer and assessing her carefully.

"It's not a daughter, it is a son," Pem told him confidently.

"I seriously doubt it, that is not the way of things. As a vampire you will see that nothing here is left to chance. You've had a boy so your next child is destined to be a girl."

"I have no idea of the way of things, I simply know what my heart has told me. It has told me that I am carrying a son."

"Well if that is true it is all the better than. It will be good to have a true Milan son in the line, in the event that anything ever happens to Alexander," said Salinar, flashing her the tiniest bit of a sly smile.

"Salinar, you promised if you gave my son your name he would be safe," snapped Pem.

"He is safe, for now. Though you must realize I have no control over what the lad does once he reaches legal age."

Pem glared at him, if anything ever happened to her son she would never forgive him.

"For now I am most interested in spending a bit of time with my new wife," he said, flashing her a sly smile.

"Why would you want to spend time with me, when you have courtesans who can meet your every need!" snapped Pem.

"I haven't touched a slut in weeks! What is wrong with you?"

"A young beautiful maiden came to my room this evening, she blushed when I mentioned your name."

"Perhaps she has heard the rumors of my size. I have heard that the rumors, which are only slightly exaggerated, cause all the young maidens to quiver at the thought of feeling a man so large as me, inside them."

"I imagine that since they don't know you personally, it might seem exciting, to have relations with a man the size of a small tree trunk."

"You obviously enjoyed yourself," he laughed a bit as he moved closer to her.

"As I said before, you are wasting your time. I am already pregnant. It is not necessary for you to spend any more time with me. Our kingdom now has the heir they need."

"And what about my needs?" Salinar was inching closer by the second.

"I care not about your needs, let your courtesans do what they do, I don't care!" snapped Pem.

"Obviously you do, or you wouldn't keep bringing them up."

"Get out of my room!" snapped Pem.

"What is wrong with you!" cried Salinar, suddenly grabbing her by both arms and pushing her against the wall with all his strength. Pem gasped as she hit the wall and soon he was pressing his body suggestively against hers.

"Let me go!"

"You are my wife," said Salinar, his face was so close to hers, his breath was washing over her, causing her to shiver.

"I am already pregnant. If you want me so bad I suggest you get out your chains."

Pem was angry, but she was only half joking, something was telling her, as she said the words, he wouldn't hesitate for a moment to get out the chains.

"A splendid idea," said Salinar, waving his arm like a maestro leading a symphony.

In seconds Pem was restrained on the bed, naked, spread eagle and once again in irons. She gasped when she realized he was going to be in complete control over her, once again.

"I'm very sorry my darling, but it was you who suggested it," he told her, flashing her a sly smile.

"You are the most obnoxious..."

"Please, please. I've had enough of your insults. If you are so worried about the damn courtesans, I will let you be one. I am your Lord and Master and you will pleasure me, without receiving pleasure yourself, do you understand?"

Pem narrowed her eyes at him. How could she possibly be married this man who she detested so much.

"I will remind you that your son is still at my disposal, so I suggest that you be nice. If I like your efforts, perhaps I will pleasure you as well.

Pem glared at him as he crawled onto the bed. He was smiling that evil smile. He knew she would do whatever he asked of her, Alexander's life was completely in his hands.

"This might be just a bit awkward, with you in irons, but since you seem to be the only woman in this kingdom who can actually handle it, I want you to suck my cock," he said straddling her face and placing his thick cock into her mouth.

It was hard in this position, but Pem had done it before, despite the fact that he was so large. She was determined to just get this over with. She couldn't hold him with her hands to control how deeply she was going to take him into her mouth, so he was in complete control. She had her lips around him and was taking him into her mouth a little bit at a time until she soon had his entire, huge cock in her mouth and her throat.

At first, he was sliding in and out in a slow, gentle rhythm, but as he got more excited his thrusts were getting faster. Soon, Pem could feel him getting even harder until he spasmed, shooting his cum all over the back of her throat. He smiled at her in approval as she sucked it all down.

"How do you like being a courtesan my love? Giving pleasure but not receiving it? I confess it sounds a bit boring to me."

Pem rolled her eyes.

"Wouldn't you rather be my wife?'

"No, not really," snapped Pem, angrily.

"Are you sure it wouldn't it be a bit more fun, if you could have a glorious orgasm as well?"

"You got what you wanted, go away," snapped Pem.

"You are so unbelievably stubborn. I have only just begun, my darling. The evening is quite young and we have all night. We are newlyweds, everyone expects us to enjoy the pleasures of each other's bodies." said Salinar.

He kissed her, then he began trailing kisses down her neck to her breasts, where he paused and slowly sucked each

nipple till they were swollen and rock hard. Pem was trying to resist him, but soon she could feel her entire body shaking with desire. There was no use pretending she didn't want him, he was going to figure it out momentarily.

He trailed kisses down her abdomen and worked his way slowly down to the soft mound of hair between her legs.

"Ready my love?' he called, flashing her a sly smile before he ducked his face between her legs. He carefully used one both hands to spread her apart before testing the waters with one finger. Pem let out a gasp and moaned, arching her body toward his hand. In moments he had his whole face between her legs. Pem was writhing uncontrollably as he used his tongue, his lips and his teeth to make her have one orgasm after another. Just when she thought she couldn't possibly cum anymore he knelt between her legs and pushed the tip of his rock hard cock into her.

Pem arched her back in an attempt to pull him in deeper, but he was playing with her, he was holding back, enjoying the wet, sucking sound of his cock sliding around her wet slit. He would only allow the head of his cock barely inside of her, making her completely mad with wanting.

"Please," cried Pem, arching her back more, straining against the irons in an attempt to push him completely inside her.

"What do you want my darling?" teased Salinar, slowly rubbing his rock hard cock against her clit, causing her to moan and convulse with ecstasy.

"Oh God, just do it!" cried Pem, she was completely breathless.

"Do you want my cock in you?" breathed Salinar, he wanted to hear her say it.

"Yes! Yes!" cried Pem, she couldn't help it, she couldn't take it anymore.

Salinar let it slide in agonizingly slow, Pem was shaking uncontrollably right on the edge of an orgasm, she was willing him to slam his cock in to the hilt and take her over the edge. When he was just halfway in Salinar began to slowly withdraw, Pem arched her back in response, afraid he was going to completely withdraw, she wasn't sure she could take it. With that he rammed into her so hard, her body began spasming with a powerful climax immediately. Salinar then began to rock on top of her in a rhythm that would cause them both to climax soon.

When he finally exploded inside her Pem came again, her entire body shaking uncontrollably. Salinar released the irons and took her into his arms, cradling her there gently. Pem was struggling to catch her breath.

"Did you enjoy yourself, my love?' he asked, his breath was hot in her ear.

"How could I not?" she gave him a sincere smile, she had never in her life experienced orgasms like that. Her entire body felt as if it was glowing from the sensation.

"I'm glad. I just want you to love me," said Salinar.

"I do, I just get so angry when I think about you with another woman."

"But you are the one I married, you are the one I want forever."

"But you married me because you had to, because I have Venezia blood, not because you wanted me."

"I swear to you, I have never wanted anyone more than I wanted you. Did you not feel it when we made love?"

Pem smiled, finally. "I did."

"Well are you finally going to shut up about sluts," asked Salinar, his voice was slightly sarcastic.

Pem sighed. "Probably not."

CHAPTER SEVENTEEN

Later that evening Pem and Salinar were to spend their first evening at court as a married couple. Since she'd arrived at the castle Pem had only been to court once. She'd spent most of her time in solitary confinement. She'd been presented at court one time, as Salinar's fiancee, but that was all she knew of the social convention the royals called court.

As King and Queen consort, Pem and Salinar were now head of the royal court and therefore they would be destined to spend a great deal of time there, socializing with their peers and their subjects.

Salinar had returned to his chambers and Pem's maid was fussing anxiously over her hair and her jewels, wanting to make her look perfect for her official appearance at court.

Pem was wearing a crimson velvet gown with a low cut square neckline that hugged, but barely concealed her breasts. The narrow bodice hugged her still tiny waist, but she was but a day pregnant. Vampire pregnancies advanced quickly, this dress wouldn't fit her long.

Pem met Salinar on the balcony and they made their arrival in the grand hall of the castle to the blare of trumpets. The entire crowd applauded in welcome as they walked regally to their thrones.

After formal court, Pem and Salinar were free to mingle in the large crowd. Pem was busy meeting members of the court. Salinar slowly followed behind, shaking hands as admirers congratulated him on his marriage. As Pem walked past a group of young women, she noticed they were giggling and she heard one of them whisper Salinar's name.

Pem gave them a suspicious glare and they all bowed regally to her.

Pem couldn't help it, she could only imagine that one or more of those women had intimate knowledge of her husband as a courtesan.

As daylight approached the crowd began to break up. Salinar took his wife by the arm to escort her to her chambers. When they reached her room he smiled at her.

"May I come in?" he asked.

"I"d rather you didn't," snapped Pem angrily.

"What's wrong? Did you not have a good time tonight?"

"It's bad enough for me, without all the women giggling and whispering your name," snapped Pem.

"Do you believe I was the only one they were whispering about?" asked Salinar, raising his eyebrows at her.

"No, I imagine not," sighed Pem. "It just drives me crazy, I can't stop thinking about you with someone else."

"Do you think I don't imagine you with Fortuno?"

"I'm not minimizing your pain, but Fortuno is dead, I could never be with him again, even if I wanted to. These women though...it seems like they're everywhere."

"I am not really as exciting as you think. Have I laid with others? You've caught me, so of course I can't deny it, but I have not since then. What can I do to make you believe me?"

"I believe you," said Pem, frowning slightly.

"Then what?" cried Salinar, his frustration growing.

"I don't know," sighed Pem, closing the door between her and Salinar.

She couldn't help it, she wanted to be alone in her chambers, not making love to a husband she suspected of having dozens of lovers on the side.

She knew he was disappointed, but she couldn't help it. Watching all the women at court as they watched Salinar had only made it worse. He was handsome, in a severe kind of way and he had power, what woman could resist that? He merely had to wave his arm and he could have whatever woman he wanted. Pem was beginning to think it would be much nicer to be married to a nobody.

Pem slept all day, being pregnant was exhausting, even though she really wasn't that far along. The last rays of the sunset were casting a deep orange light through the room and she was pacing nervously, as she was so hungry for blood, she could barely stand it another second. She heard a rap at the door and she commanded the knocker to enter.

The young maid was standing before her with her tray. Pem took the goblet from the tray and the maid curtsied and turned to leave the room.

"Wait!' cried Pem. The young woman stopped, but did not turn around.

Pem strolled around till she was standing in front of this young woman. The woman was beautiful with flawless porcelain skin and auburn hair that had been braided and twisted into a bun at the back of her head.

"Yesterday, when I mentioned Salinar's name you giggled and blushed, why?" snapped Pem.

The young woman's serene face was suddenly panicked.

"I'm sorry your Majesty. I could not help it, I have heard the rumors, when you mentioned his name it made me think of them." breathed the poor nervous maid, her face was red with shame.

"What rumors?"

"Not rumors so much, it was what was told to us by Serina, she was his concubine, before he married. She found herself pregnant with his child and she was well aware that she would burn...for loosing her self control and getting pregnant..."

"Yes, what else did she say?"

The poor maid looked so nervous, Pem thought she might pass out.

"She said she would never regret being with him like that. She told us that his cock was as big a jousting lance." the maid looked away, her face a bright shade of red. "I couldn't help but think about that when I you spoke his name. I mean, you being his wife and all..."

"And have you personal knowledge, of his size?"

"Oh no your Majesty! I would be quite intimidated to come upon a man of that size, I'm not sure I could handle it!"

"Well, I dare say that rumors of his size have been greatly exaggerated. If I were ever to be impaled on a jousting lance, I feel I might be too ruined to ever have sex again," said Pem dryly.

The maid giggled in embarrassment.

"Is that all, your Majesty?"
"Yes, but no more speculating about my husband please. I fear I cannot help but be a jealous wife."

"Yes, my lady," said the maid, as she quickly curtsied out the door.

Salinar arrived shortly after so they could attend their second night of court. After formal court they mingled in the crowd again. Unfortunately, she couldn't help noticing the adoring glances, blushes and whispers among the ladies whenever Salinar passed by. He never acknowledged any of the ladies, but Pem couldn't help it, she was jealous all the same.

Salinar was leading her towards a group of men.

"I wish for you to meet my brother. He has been staying in a distant Kingdom and he only recently returned. He is quite anxious to meet you," said Salinar, smiling at her.

Pem could only nod at him. She hadn't even realized he had a brother, so this was a bit of a surprise. They approached the group of men who were deep in a discussion of coven politics, when they saw Salinar and Pem they turned all their attention on their approaching monarchy by bowing deeply.

Pem nodded regally to the group, as Salinar introduced them all, one by one.

"Lastly, I am very pleased to introduce you to my brother Persius of Milan," said Salinar, bowing to the man that was standing there.

Pem sank into a deep curtsy as the man bowed respectfully to her.

"Your Majesty," he said, in a deep, musical voice.

"So good to meet you Persius, until this evening I was not even aware that Salinar had a brother," said Pem, smiling at him.

"He likes to hide my existence most times, since I am much better looking than he is," said Persius, flashing her a devilish smile.

"My dear brother, as charming as you are, I must ask that you stop flirting with my wife. I cannot have you mesmerizing her with both your good looks and your charm," said Salinar, ribbing his brother good naturedly.

Pem was glancing over Salinar's long lost brother carefully. It was obvious they were brothers as Persius looked a great deal like his brother Salinar. Persius was tall and muscular with dark hair that fell rakishly over one eye. He was definitely more handsome than Salinar, he looked friendlier, not quite as severe looking as his stern faced brother. He had kind eyes and an easy smile.

"I must say, I have heard nothing but praise about the beauty and intellect of my brother's new wife," said Persius.

"Obviously, it was someone other than your brother who told you these things. Salinar thinks I'm as stupid as a rock," said Pem.

"Actually, my brother has told me that you are not only the most beautiful woman he has ever met, but he feels you are so clever, he might find himself in possession of a wife he cannot control."

"Well, that part is probably true," Pem giggled, flashing her husband a smug smile.

"Perhaps my brother will team up with me, in an sincere effort to finally get you under control," said Salinar, flashing her a meaningful smile, though Pem wasn't quite sure what he was getting at.

They spent the rest of the evening socializing with Persius and the rest of the court, Pem was finding Persius very charming and knowledgable about most things in their kingdom, despite his extended absence. When the first light of dawn finally began shine through the leaded glass windows of the great hall, their little crowd dispersed to their chambers.

When they reached the top of the stairs, Salinar guided Pem toward his own chambers and this time, she didn't resist him. She felt a bit better about their relationship tonight, knowing that most of the giggling she heard about her husband was related to rumors of his exaggerated size and she was honestly surprised that Salinar had spoken so favorably of her to his brother.

They entered Salinar's room and as soon as the door had closed behind them, he took her into his arms and kissed her deeply. Pem kissed him back passionately, pressing her body against his, silently urging him on.

In moments Salinar had pushed her back onto the bed and was feverishly undressing her.

"What's this, no chains?" teased Pem.

"Do I need them?"

"I've heard all the rumors about you, I merely wish to confirm them," said Pem, giggling.

"What rumors are these?"

"Rumors of your size, my Lord," giggled Pem

"Oh, you mean the rumors going around that say that my cock is the size of a small tree trunk."

"No my Lord, the ones who say you are the size of a jousting lance."

"A jousting lance? That does sound impressive. Are you certain you can handle a man of such great size?" he teased.

"I'm willing to die trying," said Pem, sliding her hand down the front of his pants.

CHAPTER EIGHTEEN

Pem was busy with preparations for the upcoming coronation. By the end of the week her and Salinar would officially be King and Queen consort of their kingdom. Pem delighted in the feeling of her son moving inside her and her abdomen seemed to be growing each day. She had so many things she needed to do, but it seemed she tired so easily.

Pem was hurrying down the torchlit corridor to meet with the seamstress that would make her elaborate gown for the coronation. As she hurried down the corridor, she passed a group of three maids who were gossiping just outside one of the doorways.

As Pem passed by, they all giggled and she once again heard her husband's name whispered. She spun around and approached them, the giggling ended abruptly as the maids all blushed and looked away in embarrassment.

"What are you three giggling about!" she demanded.

"Nothing your Majesty," said one of the girls nervously.

"You had to be giggling about something. Normally I wouldn't care, but I could have sworn I heard someone whisper the name Salinar."

The maids were all anxiously staring at their feet, unwilling to look her in the eye.

"Which one of you said it?" snapped Pem.

"It was I, your Majesty," said the tallest of them. She was pale blonde and washed out looking.

"Tell me what you said to make these other ladies giggle."

"Only that Lady Moira had been bragging of his great size."

"Lady Moira?"

"My Lady, the Marquess."

"Does your lady claim to have firsthand knowledge of his size?"

"Yes, your Majesty. She told me she was with him two nights ago and she rode him like a stallion. She feared after that experience, she might walk bow legged the rest of her life."

The maid blushed and looked away again. Pem was stewing barely concealed anger.

"That is all, be on your way," snapped Pem who was now debating with herself on if she should meet with the seamstress or if she should go confront her husband.

Pem sighed and went on to the chambers of the seamstress, she didn't feel like arguing anyway. It was too exhausting.

The seamstress had her dressed in her elaborate gold dress which was trimmed in lace which skimmed loosely over her stomach, so not to draw attention to her growing belly. She was measuring, pinning and jotting notes to herself on a small piece of parchment.

"I want to make sure it will still fit you on Friday. The baby is growing so quickly, I dare say it must be a boy," said the seamstress.

"My heart is telling me the same thing. Salinar says it is not the way of things. Is that bad?"

"I think it would be splendid if you had a boy. It would help to cement your place in the monarchy, having another heir with Salinar."

Pem sighed, she knew that no matter what, Alexander would always be considered a bastard, but what was done, was done. There was no changing things now.

"My Lady, what do you know of Lady Moira?" asked Pem. She couldn't take it any longer, her curiosity was killing her.

"Your Majesty, I do not care for the woman at all. She is a bitter, unhappy soul and she will do whatever she must to undo the happiness of others. I prefer to stay as far away from her as possible."

Pem let out a sigh of relief. Perhaps this little tale had been specifically designed to make it's way back to her. She had already told several people she was impossibly jealous. Once the word was out, especially among the servants, anyone could find it easy to use her jealousy to manipulate her.

"What has she done?"

"I'm not quite sure she's actually done it. I think she told one of her servants a lie, in the hopes that it would make it back to me."

"That sounds about right. May I ask what this lie was?"

"She told her maid that she had slept with my husband," breathed Pem, barely able to say the words.

"Really, and when was this?"

"Two nights ago. I feel I bit guilty, I sent him away that night, it's just that I've been so tired, maybe I..."

"Your Majesty please. You are pregnant and I believe any of his courtesans would respect that, believe me, your husband did not end up in the bed of another woman that night. I was there in his chambers most of the night as picked the fabrics for his coronation attire and yours. He is very much in love with you, I hope you know."

"I want to believe that, but I get so jealous sometimes, just knowing that he's been with other women."
"Don't think me to be impertinent, but do not be such a hypocrite, you have a child by another man, your Majesty."

"I know, but that seems different. We were married, I thought I would be with Fortuno forever. I haven't been with another man since I've been betrothed to Salinar, but he has been with other women."

"Would you feel better if you were to have an affair?" asked the woman, giving her a sly smile.

"No, that's ridiculous! I mean we're married now, that would be adultery."

"Well just so you know, our world is a little different than the civilized world you came from. Vampires for the most part, are not quite as monogamous as mortals. Of course, we mate for life, but as long as a union doesn't produce a child, no one here frowns upon it. Men often spend their time with courtesans and woman here feel free to have affairs when they are pregnant."

"Women have affairs when they are pregnant!" exclaimed Pem.

"Well, it's the perfect time. You can't really get more pregnant, can you?"

"I would certainly hope not," said Pem, rolling her eyes.

"Besides, pregnant women have a certain appeal to the men of our species. I've heard a man say there is nothing so satisfying as burying his cock inside a woman who is burning with a baby inside her. She feels so hot to them it's as if they will burn inside her. Once they've felt the feeling, they want it again and again."

"Well that explains a lot, Salinar is about to wear me out, making love two or three times a day."

"Take advantage of it while you can, you could probably have whatever man you wanted, right now." said the seamstress.

"But I only want Salinar. I can't seem to let go of this stupid jealousy."

"I will talk to him if you want," said the woman.

"No, that would be too embarrassing, I will deal with this myself."

Later that evening Pem found herself seated between Salinar and Persius at court. They'd been drinking wine and were both a bit drunk and they kept coming up with lame excuses to toast each other.

A little three piece band struck up a tune and many of the guests got up and began dancing.

"Your Majesty?" said Persius, bowing to her in a formal invitation to dance.

"I fear I'm getting too big, said Pem patting her swollen abdomen, I'm sure you can find another lady to dance with you."

Persius headed to the dance floor to find a dance partner and Salinar, scooted his chair a bit closer to her.

"You should have danced with him, now the fool will find some mindless wench to dance with," said Salinar, smiling at her.

"He's not married, he shall have his pick of all the mindless wenches," laughed Pem.

"Do you like him?"

"Of course I like him, he's a very nice guy," said Pem.

"Do you think he's handsome?"

"Well he does look a bit like his brother who I find quite handsome, so I guess the answer is yes."

"I trust him, you know," said Salinar, looking into her eyes very seriously.

"What do you mean?" asked Pem, suddenly worried that none of this was idle talk.

"I not only trust him with my life, I trust him with my wife."

"I'm afraid I don't follow. I think you and your brother have had a bit too much to drink. You should stick to blood, you obviously can't hold your alcohol."

"I talked to Lady Paula tonight," said Salinar, his voice was serious.

"About our Coronation attire?"

"No about Lady Moira and the rumors you heard."

"It's okay, she told me that Lady Moira is a compulsive liar, and that you were with her that night."

"I know, but she had an idea, and I think it might make you feel as if the playing field were leveled."

"I'm not quite sure I have the faintest idea what you are speaking about,"said Pem shaking her head miserably.

"Well, you are pregnant, so if you were to have an affair..."

"No Salinar, that's completely ludicrous. I really couldn't do that."

"Why not? Men enjoy courtesans without any social stigma. You could feel free to enjoy yourself without the fear of becoming pregnant."

"But I..."

"Just think about it Pem. I would support you if you wanted to spend the night with my brother. All I ask in return is that you drop this jealous wife routine and never mention the courtesans again."

"The very thought is crazy enough but really Salinar, your brother!" cried Pem, completely horrified by the thought.

"Like I said, I trust him, he's my blood and he would never betray me."

"I believe you, but there is no need. You two drunk fools need to sleep it off," said Pem shaking her head miserably.

On Friday the entire kingdom was bursting with excitement over the Coronation. Salinar and Pem rode through the torchlight streets of the Kingdom in an open carriage, just

after dusk. The formal ceremony was carried out in the church and it was so beautiful Pem was moved to tears.

Back at the castle in the main hall there was plenty of food, drink and dancing. Pem had remained at the head table for most of the festivities, she felt too awkward to dance any of festive dances in her state. Though when a waltz was signaled, it was Persius that arrived at her side to ask for a dance.

"Your Majesty," he said kissing her hand.

"I guess this one waltz won't hurt," said Pem, taking his hand and letting him lead her onto the dance floor.

In moments they were swirling gracefully on the dance floor. Pem felt as light as air in Persius' arms, not clumsy and unwieldy like she normally felt. He was holding her tightly in his arms, much closer than the rest of the dancers.

"You look very beautiful tonight, your Majesty," he told her, looking into her eyes.

"You are such a charmer when you are drunk," laughed Pem.

"I am not drunk."

"If not completely drunk, then well on your way," said Pem, giggling.

"I have to agree with that." he laughed.

Pem looked over to see Salinar dancing with a beautiful young maid.

"Who's that?" asked Pem, eyeing them suspiciously.

"Lady Olivia."

"Is she one of his sluts?'

"A former one, that much I know. I'm not sure if he's seen her recently."

"She's very pretty," said Pem, frowning.

"You know you shouldn't be jealous of the courtesans. They provide a service, that is all. For most men, my brother included, they mean absolutely nothing."

"Then why is he dancing with her?"

"Why are you dancing with me?"

"Because you asked me," said Pem, laughing.

"What if I asked you to do something else?"

"I would tell you that I am married."

"And I would tell you that your window of opportunity is small," said Persius, flashing her a sly smile.

"My window of opportunity?"

"How long till you deliver, two weeks perhaps?"

"I don't know, I still haven't figured this whole vampire pregnancy thing out."

"Vampire females are designed to reproduce. The only time you aren't fertile is when you are already pregnant. Pregnant women are infinitely fascinating to all men, because they provide the best sex ever."

"Really?"

"That's what I've heard, but I'm a single guy, so I have no real experience, but I'd be willing to try it out."

Pem pulled herself out of his arms and glared at him.

"Wait till Salinar hears you've been hitting on me!" she cried.

"We've already spoke of this, it was his suggestion," said Persius.

Pem rolled her eyes and stalked away from Persius, she couldn't believe the nerve he had, suggesting such a thing.

In a few moments Salinar had finished his dance and was standing there at her side.

"How was Lady Olivia?" snarled Pem.

"You wouldn't be jealous of that vapid little minx would you?"

"Hardly," she snapped.

"Then why are you suddenly so angry at me?"

"I'm not angry at you, I'm angry at your brother!"

"What did he do?"

"He hit on me," snapped Pem.

"I asked him to," said Salinar, rolling his eyes miserably.

"Why would you do that?"

"Your jealousy has nothing to do with me and everything to do with your own feelings."

"Are you completely mad?"

"Perhaps, but I am also right. Your jealousy tells me that it is possible you need something in your life that I cannot give you.

"And what would that be?"

"I'm not quite sure, only you can answer that question. Confidence, abandon, self awareness? What is it that you need, that I cannot give you?"

"Trust?"

"Perhaps, but I have been around many years, of course, I have been with many women. The sooner you accept that, the better.

You must realize, sexual release is merely an act. In your short lifetime you have had just two sexual partners, one you have lost, one you've pledged the rest of your life to.

I cannot help but feel that perhaps it is my many years of experience that has you feeling so jealous. Maybe a bit more experience is what you need."

"But why Persius?"

"He is my brother, he will not betray me. I have complete trust in you and Persius, trust that it will be a sexual act, not an act of love. That can only be between you and I."

"I don't think I can..."

"You will, tonight. It has all been arranged," said Salinar looking into her eyes earnestly.

"I would feel dishonest, sneaky."

"It won't be sneaky at all, I'll be watching."

"Are you completely insane?"

"Perhaps, so don't make me force the issue. There is always chains," he told her, flashing her an evil smile.

"You would place me in chains to make love to your own brother?" cried Pem.

"Not make love, have sex. There is a difference."

Pem rolled her eyes and stomped away, he was drunk and there was no reasoning with him.

When Pem returned to her chambers that evening, she firmly locked her door. She didn't trust Salinar or his horny brother and it had been a long day she was exhausted. She fell asleep quickly and awoke to a knock on her door sometime later.

"Go away," she called.

"Open this door now, or I promise, you will be sorry," snapped Salinar.

Pem sighed and got up and unlatched the door. Salinar followed her across the room.

"Why did you lock me out?" he snapped angrily.

"I wasn't sure what was wrong with you, I just wanted to be alone."

"Well not tonight. You are the kingdom's new Queen consort, I am your Lord and Master and you will do what I ask of you." said Salinar, touching her cheek softly.

Salinar took her into his arms and kissed her passionately. Pem was kissing him back as his hands moved down her body, caressing her. Pem turned around so that he could unfasten the back of her gown and she was shocked to see Persius standing there in the doorway.

Pem took a nervous step backwards and Salinar suddenly clamped both his hands on her wrists, holding her completely still.

"You will do this and you will never mention another word about my past, courtesans or lovers, do you understand, your Majesty?" he whispered angrily into her ear. Then he pushed her toward his brother.

"Do not be afraid," said Persius, smiling and holding his hand out to her.

Pem wasn't afraid, she was angry. She was suddenly determined that if this was what Salinar wanted, it was exactly what he was going to get. She was going to have sex with his brother and she was going to enjoy every last second of it. She flashed Salinar a sly smile and pushed Persius' hand away. She reached back and ripped her dress right down the back and let it fall to the floor.

Persius was staring at her with a mixture of shock and astonishment. She smiled seductively at him and stepped out of her undergarments. Pem reached up to let her hair down and it fell in loose curls over her naked breasts as Persius stood there, too shocked to move. She flashed Salinar a sly smile and crawled like a cat into the bed, motioning to Persius to come over.

Salinar's brow was suddenly wrinkled in confusion, but he stepped out of his brother's way and slowly prowled away to the dark recesses of the room, never taking his eyes off of the strange encounter in front of him.

Pem was determined to play this all out like some sort of experienced courtesan, even though she had absolutely no experience as such an experienced seductress.

She watched as Persius took off his clothes, he had a beautiful body and she didn't want to waste a single second playing the shy, inexperienced young woman. Her husband had given her quite the gift and this gift was now climbing slowly and slightly unsurely into the bed with her.

Pem had no desire to waste time with preliminaries, so when Persius tried to kiss her, she placed one finger over his lips and began trailing kisses slowly down his abdomen, till she reached her intended target.

He groaned in approval as she wrapped her fingers around his cock, which was already standing at attention. It was at least as long as Salinar's, but not near as thick. She flicked her tongue seductively across the tip and down the shaft and soon it's veins were bulging out and it was stiff as a piece of steel.

Pem smiled to herself, Salinar had probably thought there was no way she would go through with this, he was probably ready to shit himself right now. Just you wait...she thought to herself. Salinar had told her she was very skilled, being able to take his large cock in her mouth without gagging. She decided that Persius was about to be impressed as well.

In seconds she had taken his entire long cock into her mouth and was working it with everything she had. Persius was grunting like an ape and he was gasping to breathe, his hips moved faster and Pem moved faster matching his speed

until he let out an agonizing cry and shot his cum into the back of her throat, his whole body quivering in ecstasy. Pem sucked up every last drop and prepared to give him a few minutes to rest, but apparently he didn't need it.

Barely taking a moment to catch his breath, Persius flipped Pem onto her back and began kissing every square inch of her body, taking time to suck each nipple till they stood out hard and proud. He trailed kisses down her swollen abdomen, then he gently parted her, using his tongue, his lips and eventually his hands to bring her to so many orgasms she finally lost count. Her body couldn't stop it's intense shaking.

"That's enough Persius," snapped Salinar's harsh voice from the perimeter of the room.

Pem jumped a little bit, she had completely forgotten he was there, she was so consumed by his brother's talents. She almost sighed in regret, she was exhausted from her multiple orgasms, but she wasn't quite done yet, she was dying to feel Persius inside her.

"No, it's not," breathed Persius, climbing on top of her and sliding his long cock into her effortlessly.

Pem shuddered as she felt him slide into her. She was so sensitive at this point, each time he thrust into her, she felt as if her entire body was going to turn inside out. She was moaning and gasping uncontrollably. She had wanted to play the aloof courtesan, but that plan was not working out for her.

Persius was getting excited as well, he knew from Pem's shuddering body, that she was enjoying herself. Salinar had moved closer and was standing several feet from the bed with his hands on his hips, his displeasure with the situation evident.

Persius couldn't help it, his brother's stern face made him want to laugh. If Salinar was mad, that was too bad, he wasn't stopping until he was done, this had been his brother's idea. Persius had been all to happy to indulge him. He didn't plan to stop until he shot his load inside Pem's burning hot pussy, which was like nothing he had every experienced before. It was the strangest sensation of pleasure bordering on pain and the fire he felt was all consuming. Nope, no matter how envious his brother appeared, he couldn't stop now.

Pem was completely out of control, her body convulsing with one orgasm after another, her moans were so loud, Persius feared the entire kingdom could hear her.

He gave his brother a mischievous smile, as he was about to give her even more. He doubled the pace of his thrusts, ramming into his brother's wife even harder, her moans were reaching a crescendo and he was ready for release.

When he finally came inside her, Pem wrapped her legs around him holding him inside her as her entire body shook violently. They both collapsed into a pile, their ragged breaths slowly returning to normal. Salinar emerged from the shadows, his face stern and businesslike.

"Get dressed and get the hell out of here," he snapped, tossing Persius' clothing to him. Persius dressed quickly and left without another word.

"Well that was very impressive, quite the show," said Salinar, his voice was sarcastic.

Pem was still struggling to breathe. She hadn't expected to enjoy it that much. In fact, she'd thought she was in control, but it was obvious she wasn't. She'd just experienced the most consuming lovemaking she'd ever experienced. She

just wanted to lay there and bask in the glow of the intense pleasure she had just experienced.

"It was fine," snapped Pem.

"It seemed more than fine," said Salinar, unbuttoning his shirt.

"I don't know why you're so angry with me, this was what you wanted right? It was you who arranged this. I'm not a courtesan, did you think I wouldn't enjoy myself?"

"I am not quite sure what I thought. I only know that now I'm completely turned on and I'm not about to let my brother have one up on me."

"Salinar please, I'm completely exhausted."

Salinar climbed into the bed completely naked, his arousal was completely evident. Pem started to crawl away but he caught her by the waist. He lifted her hips so that she was on her knees and he took her from behind. He took her roughly, ramming into her again and again. Pem was sensitive from her previous encounter, so in seconds she was shaking with yet another orgasm. It wasn't long till Pem heard Salinar let out a loud shout as he came inside her.

He gathered Pem into his arms and promptly fell asleep. As his snores filled the room, Pem fell asleep as well, her dreams filled with thoughts of Persius.

CHAPTER NINETEEN

Pem awoke shortly before sunset. Salinar was still tangled in the sheets beside her. She looked him over carefully wondering what she needed more right now, sex or blood. She was craving both equally, but sex seemed the easiest to obtain for now. She'd forgotten that near the end of her previous pregnancy she'd grown almost insatiable. For some reason, this time seemed almost worse.

She scooted her body over to Salinar's and reached under the sheets, running her palm over the rock hard plane of his abdomen and letting it drift into the curly mass of pubic hair below.

She ran her hand down the length of his flaccid cock, which immediately began to respond to her touch. She smiled as she wrapped her fingers around his now growing cock, it truly was the largest cock she had ever seen and it continued to grow as he slowly began to wake up. As he stirred, she continued to fondle him until he was nearly his fully engorged size.

"Hmmm, somebody's horny already," he said stretching and moving closer to her.

"I cannot help it," said Pem smiling and moving her hand faster.

Salinar rolled her onto her back and kissed her deeply, poising himself to enter her.

"Can you take me from behind again? I fear my stomach is getting too big to have you on top anymore," said Pem.

"We shall do it however you wish, your Majesty," he said, pulling her to her knees by her hips. Pem shifted around till her butt was pointed toward him, instead of grabbing her hips and plunging into her like she had anticipated, he slowly dipped one finger into her, then two. Pem moaned in approval, but she was already dripping wet, she needed his cock inside her, not this beginner's foreplay.

"Fuck me Salinar," she breathed. She could barely stand this, she wanted to feel his cock buried inside her.

"I will, I just want to teach you a new trick," his voice was low and sensual.

Pem almost breathed a sigh of relief when she finally felt him scoot his body closer, he rubbed the tip of his cock up and down her dripping wet slit and across her clit, causing her to shiver and push her buttocks toward him, hoping to entice him to slide his entire cock into her.

Salinar finally pushed his cock halfway in, Pem groaned in delight, as it slid back he took two fingers already wet with her juices and slid them into her ass, causing her to shudder and moan. Soon Salinar was moving slowly within her, his fingers in her ass using the same rhythm. She was squirming uncontrollably as the feeling was something she had never experienced before. She came quickly and Salinar increased his pace to bring himself to his own orgasm.

Soon Pem was bucking like a bronco, she couldn't hold still. Salinar had to grip both her hips just to keep his cock inside her. He finally came inside her causing Pem to convulse with one final climax.

Salinar and Pem lay there tangled in the sheets, gasping to breathe. Pem started giggling.

"What are you giggling about?" asked Salinar.

"I was a little horrified when you stuck your fingers in my butt hole, I thought it was going to hurt. No one has ever done anything like that to me before. I started to protest, but it felt so good, I could only moan," said Pem laughing in embarrassment.

"I would love to fuck your ass, but I am too large. I don't think your tiny ass could take it."

"I didn't even know such a thing was possible, I would expect it would hurt, but it actually felt good, once you got going."

"Most courtesans prefer it that way, since there is no chance of getting pregnant. I'm too large though, I haven't found one who was willing to try."

"I'd be willing to try," teased Pem.

"If my cock wasn't so thick, I would definitely do it, but I truly don't want to hurt you."

"Perhaps Persius could." said Pem, her voice was hopeful. Persius was such a skilled lover, she couldn't stop thinking about him.

"What? No, I don't think so. You've had your little tryst with Persius, it's over."

"But I was thinking that..."

"What?"

"It felt so amazing to feel your fingers inside me, while your cock was inside me. It made me think how amazing it would feel to have two cocks inside me at the same time," said Pem.

"You want an orgy?"

"Not really an orgy, just you and Persius. I mean you were there last time, perhaps this time you get to join in."

"What if he doesn't go for it?"

"Then we don't do it," said Pem, but she knew he would. The orgasms she had with Persius were so strong, she just wanted to feel that feeling again. She knew this was the only way she'd get to be with Persius again.

That evening they were obligated to show up at court, otherwise Pem would have lured both men to the bedroom as soon as possible. Her body craved sex constantly and she couldn't wait until this pregnancy was over, so her brain wasn't completely mired with thoughts of when she would get her next orgasm.

Salinar and Persius were having a drink while Pem sat on the dais fanning herself in boredom as she watched everyone congregating in the main hall.

"I have a favor to ask of you," said Salinar, glancing at his brother very seriously.

"If it's anything like the last favor you asked of me, I'm in," joked Persius.

"Actually it is similar. I'm struggling to get Pem through this pregnancy, she's become so insatiable, one man is no longer enough for her."

"So I've seen," said Persius, raising his glass in a mock toast to his brother.

"So will you come to my chambers tonight? She has the urge to feel two men inside her at the same time."

"Nice! Will she be getting kinkier as the pregnancy progresses?"

"I guess we're only limited by her imagination right now, and her lack of worldliness. Luckily she's a bit inexperienced, she didn't even know it was possible, for a woman to take a cock in her ass."

"Hmmm, suppose she wants a stallion to mount her next?" laughed Persius.

"I'd actually prefer that to what I believe is coming. If she doesn't deliver soon she may want to go on a blood kill. In this day and age I fell that's a bit risky. I do not believe I feel comfortable to have my wife away from the castle, searching for a mortal to slake her lust for sex and blood. I'll do my best to keep her satisfied in other ways, even if I must use my own brother to help me."

"I can't think of a better way to be used," said Persius, flashing his brother a sly smile.

The evening was still young when they finally abandoned court for the privacy of Salinar's chambers. Salinar wanted to satisfy his wife, but he did not want to lose control of the situation. He would do what his wife wanted, but he was in charge.

It was awkward, he wasn't sure how to start. Pem was staring them both down as if they were her prey and Persius was hanging back near the doorway, not sure how to break the awkward silence.

Salinar went to Pem and took both of her hands in his.

"I think it should begin between us, Persius can join in later."

Pem nodded as Salinar led her to the bed and took her into his arms. He was kissing her and caressing her while Persius stood awkwardly by the door.

In moments Salinar had rolled onto his back and was pulling Pem on top of him.

"I think it will work best with you on top of me, then Persius can enter you from behind."

Pem crawled on top of Salinar and slid herself down onto his fully erect cock. She sighed in ecstasy as he slid full length into her. Persius was anxiously undressing.

Pem was excited to be on top for once, usually Salinar insisted on being on top. Finally, for once she was in control. She was setting the pace, teasing her husband a little bit. She didn't want him to cum too soon. She wanted to draw this little encounter out as long as she could.

She was moving on top of Salinar slowly at first, using all her muscles to control him. She motioned for Persius to come over to her. She admired his naked body in the moonlight as he walked over to her. She had him stand in front of her so she could suck his cock.

It was amazing to be making love to her husband, but to also have another man's cock in her mouth. Both men were grunting in ecstasy. Pem knew what she needed to do. She whispered to Persius that she wanted to feel his cock in her ass.

Persius moved around till he was behind her, she paused for a moment as he slid in halfway. Pem groaned, Persius wasn't as large as Salinar, but he was still large.

"Are you okay?" he gasped.

"Do it," she gasped.

Persius didn't delay, he pushed his cock in firmly as Salinar resumed his thrusting. Pem could barely stand it once both men were moving inside her, it was like nothing she had ever experienced before. She climaxed with a loud shout as she convulsed into spams. Both men were still moving within her and she couldn't even think. She was so full she felt as if she might burst. It was a fine line between pleasure and pain and her entire body wouldn't stop shaking.

Both men had got into a rhythm, their thrusts completely matched up. Persius was fondling her breasts from behind as he rammed into her again and again. Salinar's face revealed that he was very close to orgasm. He finally exploded inside her and Pem collapsed on his chest with a powerful orgasm of her own. Seconds later Perisus let out a loud shout and climaxed as well. They all collapsed in the bed, their bodies shaking and their breathing labored.

As soon as they'd recovered, Salinar asked Persius to get dressed and leave. Pem was a bit disappointed, she had hoped they could do it again when they recovered a bit.

Salinar just wanted Persius out of the room, he'd had several woman at a time in his bed in the past, but he wasn't comfortable with another man being there. Besides, Pem had already gotten what she wanted, there was no reason to let Persius stay.

Persius was smiling to himself as he walked down the torchlit corridor to his room. He had never met a woman as insatiable as Pem. Sure he'd heard of woman having increased sexual appetites during pregnancy, but his brother definitely had his hands full with her.

When Salinar had recovered a bit he rang for the maid. She arrived carrying a tray with their blood. Pem devoured hers ravenously and asked for another. She drank that one greedily as well. When the maid was gone she reached under the sheets for Salinar again. In moments she had him hard again.

"You my darling, are the horniest thing I've ever seen. The other sluts of this kingdom have nothing on you," joked Salinar.

"Can Persius come back?"

"No, I think I got this," said Salinar, steadying her hips with his hands as she crawled in front of him on all fours.

Pem moaned as he slid his huge cock into her. They made love at least four more times before the sun came up. Salinar was exhausted. When he finally awoke the sun was setting and Pem was standing at the window looking out as darkness fell over the kingdom.

"What is the matter my darling?" asked Salinar.

"Nothing is enough any more."

"What?"

"No matter what I do I'm never satisfied, no matter how much blood I drink, my body craves more, no matter how much I enjoy our lovemaking, it's never enough. Even with Persius involved, it still wasn't enough."

"I know darling. You're nearing the end of your pregnancy, that's just how it is. Soon our son will be born and you will get back to normal."

"I can't have the baby soon enough to get rid of this feeling. Nothing will ever satisfy me again."

"Oh darling, I'm so sorry. I know what you need, I guess there is no getting around it."

"What do I need Salinar?"

"You need to kill."

CHAPTER TWENTY

The bad thing about being a part of a highly advanced vampire coven was that one could never really get past their primitive base needs. The one thing that made them immortal was the thing that made them animalistic and crude, it was their ongoing need for blood.

The coven had grown more sophisticated over the last thousand years. A small portion of the population was tasked with the killing and those of high rank did not need to worry about where their next drop of blood was coming from.

It was conditions like pregnancy that tended to throw a vampire right back to the dark ages as their ancient cravings returned like a fire that could never be extinguished.

It was a known fact, some pregnancies went on without incident, but there were some women though who couldn't shake their ancient instincts. Their bodies needed to kill, to fulfill an ancient prophecy that in modern times seemed like a bad dream.

Pem was suffering from an ancient craving her body needed to fulfill. She needed blood, and she needed to kill for it. It was dangerous, not just for Pem, but her coven. Any kill she made would need to be covered up, today's society would freak out if they suddenly began encountering the carnage of a vampire kill.

Salinar was frowning. Pem needed to kill and he was obligated to help her. He had invited Persius to his chambers for a drink. He had no doubt his brother would help him to carry out this slightly distasteful task.

"It's gotten as bad as I feared with Pem. Blood cannot satisfy her, sex cannot either. We need to arrange a blood kill for her, ASAP."

"How will you cover it up?" asked Persius.

"Modern man is stupid. It will be easy enough to make it look like an accident. I only hope that one blood kill will be enough to hold her over till the baby is born."

"I agree," said Persius.

Persius and Salinar began plotting Pem's kill. They would bring her victim here to the castle, for privacy. Later, they could arrange the victim's accidental death and no one would be the wiser.

First, Salinar would have to find a mortal man Pem would actually be interested in coupling with. When she was finished with him she would kill him and drain his blood. With any luck, it would be enough to hold her till the end of her pregnancy.

Persius and Salinar went on a mission looking for a potential victim. They needed a man, but not just any man would do. Pem would need to find him physically attractive. They arrived in the city early that evening, not really sure where to look.

They walked the putrid streets of the city. Salinar was ultimately happy he would be able to return to his own kingdom and leave behind the squalor of the mortal's city.

They crossed a busy street and came upon a gym. It looked to be full of men. Salinar thought if they could somehow lure a man into the alley, they could bite him and disable him until they got him back to their kingdom.

Persius stood there on the street corner keeping a sharp eye on the clientele, while Salinar waited in the alley.

A few guys walked out, they were just average looking guys, then Persius saw exactly what they were looking for. The next man to walk out of the gym was tall and muscular, he looked like a greek God, he had no doubt this man was attractive enough he would pique Pem's interest.

"Can you help me? Some guy just tried to rape my girlfriend," cried Persius, as the man stepped onto the sidewalk.

Persius ran into the alley with the man right behind him. The man was now looking around for the girlfriend or a crime scene, but he saw nothing. Before he knew what was happing, Salinar had moved out of the shadows and sunk his teeth into him, just enough to disable him for the trip back to the castle.

Salinar and Persius brought the man to Pem's chambers. He was drugged enough that he would never even know what had hit him.

"Look darling, I brought you a present. This is what you need to quench all your desires," said Salinar as he led the man into her chambers.

The man was gorgeous, though a bit drugged in appearance. He was manly and muscular enough, for a mere mortal.

Pem smiled as she took the man by the hand and led him to her bed. She hadn't smelled the appetizing smell of a human man since she'd made her transition, all the blood she'd consumed since she'd become a vampire had been brought to her. She'd never experienced the thrill of a blood kill. It would be like being the ultimate black widow.

Pem breathed deeply, now that she smelled human flesh, it would be impossible to turn off her need for this man's blood.

The man was pleasantly pliable, made possible by some strange concoction of drugs Salinar had poured into him. He went willingly to be with Pem and let her undress him. Pem could barely wait to get her hands on him. The man was quite drugged, so his head bobbed a bit but when she touched him he responded without any issue.

Pem reached eagerly for his cock, it was a nice size, nowhere near the size of Salinar or Persius, but it would have to do. The man was attempting to speak but his slurred speech was annoying her, she didn't have time for his babbling. Pem pushed the man back on the bed and straddled him sliding his fully erect cock inside her. She began moving slowly and deliberately, mortal men lacked self control and she wanted to make this last.

As her pace increased, the man seemed close to climaxing. Pem slowed her pace a little bit, hoping to extend her own pleasure. Though just the smell of his mortal flesh was driving her completely insane, in a few moments she was bucking and rocking on top of him like a woman out of control, when he finally came inside her, she came as well, sinking her teeth into his neck at the same time. She drank every last drop of his blood, finally satisfied...

CHAPTER TWENTY ONE

Pem lay in her bed savoring the feeling of her delightfully full belly and her body which finally felt marvelously spent. The sun was just rising and Salinar and Persius had left to dispose of the man's body.

For the first time in days Pem finally fell asleep and didn't awaken until the sun had already set. She was laying in her bed, tangled in the sheets and still completely naked.

When the men returned to the castle Salinar returned to his chambers, exhausted from their escapades outside the castle. Persius, on the other hand, was anxious to see how Pem was doing. He crept slowly down the torchlit hallway, watching for servants that might be hiding in the shadows. It might seem unseemly that he was on his way to the Queen's bedchambers unaccompanied by her husband.

He knocked lightly on the door, so not to call attention to himself, but there was no answer. He wondered if Pem had gotten up and gone to court alone. He opened the door a little bit and saw the light of several dozen candles illuminating the room. Pem was laying back in the bed tangled among the satin sheets, she was casually rubbing her nipples. She looked so lovely he couldn't help himself, he let himself into the room.

Pem startled when she saw him standing there, but didn't make any move to cover her naked body with the sheets. Her pregnant body looked voluptuous and ripe in the candlelight. Persius was already fighting an erection, and losing the battle by the second.

"Persius what a nice surprise, I had imagined it was Salinar," said Pem, her voice was hard to read, she wasn't exactly disappointed.

"I'm sorry your Majesty, I wanted to check on you and see if there was anything I could do for you," said Persius. He felt a bit embarrassed as he took a few steps into the room. The Queen was laying in her bed completely naked in the candlelight and he couldn't take his eyes off of her, he was completely mesmerized, by the sight of her body that was ripe with her pregnancy.

"Where is my husband?"

"He has gone on to his chambers, he was tired," said Persius.

"Well, in that case, come here. There is no use wasting that lovely erection."

Persius looked down in embarrassment at the bulge that was threatening to burst through his pants. He couldn't ignore that he was aroused by the sight of her, but he didn't think he could do what she wished, she was his brother's wife.

"But..."

"I appreciate your loyalty to your brother, but I need you right now. Pregnancy has cursed me with these inconceivable cravings that seem to control me. Besides, it is safe for us now. I can't get pregnant," said Pem, smiling at him.

"I'm sorry your Majesty...I can't," said Persius, turning and heading to the door.

"Please Persius, come to my bed and make love to me. My husband does not love me. But you do, I know you do," pleaded Pem.

Persius turned around and looked at her. She looked so beautiful, and he did love her. Unfortunately, she was his brother's wife, he couldn't do what she wanted him to do.

He turned abruptly and let himself out of the room. He walked quickly down the torchlit hallway, he had to get far away before he did the unthinkable.

Pem sighed miserably, she'd had vivid dreams all night and they had all been of Persius. She had been daydreaming of him and mindlessly caressing herself when he walked in. He had wanted her too, that much was perfectly obvious, but apparently his conscience got the best of him.

Persius returned to his chambers where he proceeded to pace about nervously. He wanted Pem and she wanted him, what was wrong with him?

She was right, Salinar cared about her, but did he love her? Persius wasn't sure, he did know his brother would do whatever it took to return the Milan family to the throne. True love wasn't really on his radar. He merely tolerated his strong willed wife so that their children might someday ascend to the throne.

Persius adored Pem and it had taken every ounce of self control he had within his body to walk out of that room. Now he was having second thoughts. What harm would it do? Pem was already pregnant, her body so alive and ripe she was completely insatiable in her desire.

Persius had made up his mind, he would do it. He opened the door to the torchlit corridor and stepped out into the drafty coolness.

He kept mostly in the shadows, he didn't want anyone to see him, though the corridors were deserted as everyone else must be at court. He had paused outside her chambers for

a moment to gather his nerve when he heard Pem giggling. He stepped a bit closer to the door so he could listen better, then he heard Pem moaning softly.

He frowned slightly, Salinar must not have been as exhausted as he had let on, thought Persius. He stood there for a few more moments, just listening. He could hear the soft babble of voices, but not Salinar...it almost sounded like another woman.

Persius was suddenly intrigued. He opened the door, just a bit, to peek in. His erection returned almost immediately when he realized that the person in bed with Pem was a woman, not a man. Pem was moaning and writhing as her servant girl eagerly went down on her.

Persius couldn't help himself, he opened the door a bit more, completely mesmerized by the scene in front of him.

Pem was moaning and nearing a crescendo and Persius couldn't take his eyes off of them. He had never seen a woman go down on another woman and he found the prospect positively titillating.

Pem finally climaxed, thrashing wantonly in the sheets. She finally lay there gasping to breathe, a sated smile on her face.

"Come in Persius," he heard her say, snapping him from his trancelike state.

Persius jumped at bit. He had not even realized he had let himself into the room and was staring at the scene in front of him, his erection nearly bulging out of his pants.

"Come here, I'm not too tired to give you the relief you seek."

He took a few steps toward the bed. Pem's servant gave him a nod and picked her clothing up from the floor and went into the adjoining room.

"Are you shocked to find me in bed with a woman?"

"A bit, perhaps," said Persius, desperately trying to keep his voice flat and smooth. He was nervous and there was no disguising it. Nervous about being there, nervous about seeing what he had just seen.

"When your very life has become so miserable, you do what you must to make it tolerable," said Pem.

Persius just stood there staring, he wasn't sure what to say, or if he should say anything.

"I cannot wait for this pregnancy to be over, it seems like one moment I feel perfectly sated and at peace, the next moment I feel I must get satisfaction however possible, it's a bit unnerving."

"Yes.."

"Please Persius, don't just stand there, come into the bed with me."

Persius was shaking his head, this just wasn't right.

"It's why you came back, isn't it?"

Persius took another cautious step toward her bed. His brother would murder him if he found him here. It was one thing to get him involved in a threesome, but he was certain if Salinar was to find him here in bed with his wife, he would burn.

"Yes."

"Did you change your mind again? You don't want me?"

Persius walked quickly to the bed and undressed, in moments he was tangled in her arms kissing her with wild abandon. He wanted to taste every inch of her, her ripe breasts, her rounded stomach, her juicy pussy.

Pem was moaning as he kissed her breasts taking each nipple into his mouth and sucking it greedily. His hand had slid down between her legs causing her to gasp and buck like a wild horse.

Finally, he rolled onto his back positioning her on top of him. She let him slide slowly into her before she began moving in her own rhythm on top of him. In just moments he was thrusting himself inside her as hard as he could and she was convulsing in an orgasm.

When she had finished he pushed her off and turned her around so he could take her from behind. She was bucking so deliriously he had to hold tight to her hips to keep himself inside her. She came three more times before he finally let himself release inside her and they both collapsed on the bed.

He gathered her into his arms and they both fell asleep. Just before she succumbed to her exhaustion Pem whispered in his ear.

"I love you Persius."

CHAPTER TWENTY TWO

When Pem finally awoke, she was still tangled in the sheets with Persius. She was panicking a little bit, she hadn't meant to fall asleep with her brother in law in her bed. What if Salinar came to her room?

Unfortunately, she couldn't shake her desire for him. Persius looked so appetizing laying there next to her. He was sleeping, his face looked gentle, his hair was tousled and the flat plane of his abdomen was beaconing for her to slide her hand down it to that place that was just hidden by the sheets, that she would love to arouse again. Alas, it was too dangerous. Salinar would, no doubt, be up soon.

"Persius," whispered Pem, shaking him a bit.

He opened his eyes and smiled at her.

"You look so beautiful with your hair all messed up like that," he mumbled.

"You have to go, the sun is setting," said Pem, anxiously.

Persius got up reluctantly and got dressed. As he stepped into the drafty corridor, he heard the sound of footsteps just coming around the corner from the north hallway. He backed down the corridor a bit and into the shadows.

He had escaped just in time, it was Salinar. He rapped on the door of his wife's chambers and then stepped inside. Persius let out a sigh of relief as he crept back to his own chambers on the other side of the castle.

"Hello darling," said Salinar as he stepped into Pem's chambers.

She was sitting up in bed, brushing her golden blonde locks. She was naked, but had the satin sheets just pulled over her ripe breasts. He smiled, it wouldn't be long now.

"Good evening, my Lord," she told him with a smile.

"I'm sorry I missed you last night. I was quite tired. Persius and I had to dispose of your blood kill. I should not let it bother me but I absolutely despise going into the city."

"I appreciate your efforts my Lord. I feel so much better now."

"I imagine you do. Did you sleep well your Majesty?"

"I did."

"I thought I might join you in bed, before we go to court," said Salinar, raising his eyebrows at her.

Pem almost sighed, the thought didn't sound all that exciting, even though she would have gladly made love to Persius again. It was odd, her own husband wanted to make love to her and yet it seemed like a chore. She knew she must give in to him, lest he be suspicious.

She smiled and pulled back the sheets in invitation. Salinar eagerly undressed and joined her in bed.

They made love and though she climaxed and Salinar probably had the largest cock of any man she had ever seen, it seemed strangely unsatisfying.

Afterwards they dressed and went to court. The great hall was crowded with many people. They were all socializing and dancing, but there was one person Pem couldn't keep her eyes off of. It was Persius. He looked so handsome in

his gold trimmed burgundy tunic, his hair falling rakishly over one eye.

He was quite popular in court and always had crowds of woman eager to converse with him. Pem couldn't help but feel jealous as she watched the other women crowding around and flirting with him. She smiled to herself when she realized she knew him a lot more intimately than those women ever would. She had touched every inch of his muscular body and felt his shudders as he came inside her.

When it was nearly dawn, Salinar took her by her hand to walk her back to her chambers, she was slyly hoping that he would leave and Persius would return to her, but it was not to be. As they reached the top of the stairs her body was racked with a terrible pain. It was time, she was in labor...

Hours passed and Pem labored in her bed, her maid dabbing her forehead with a cool cloth and Salinar holding her hand, mumbling encouraging words. Just when Pem had decided she was going to die, the midwife arrived and kicked Salinar out of the room.

"No!' cried Pem. She didn't want him to leave. But the midwife was steadfast, men had no place in a delivery.

"Men cannot, nor will they ever be able to handle the sight of a delivery. We are not human you know. believe me, it's better they don't see it, it would be scary as hell to them," said the midwife, placing an acrid smelling cloth over Pem's face.

Pem wrinkled her nose up and tried to push away the offensive, malodorous cloth, but it was too late, she was out.

Sometime later Pem awoke in her bed. Her pain had ceased and her breathing had returned to normal. The room was empty again and her stomach was, once again flat. She

had delivered. She felt her stomach growl with hunger pangs. She rang for her maid. The woman arrived and smiled at her.

"Is her Majesty hungry?" asked the woman, with a smile.

"Yes, but where is my baby?"

"With his wet nurse, the baby was very hungry as well," said the maid.

Pem cringed, she wasn't exactly happy with having a stranger breastfeed her baby, but she'd been told that is just how Royalty does it."

In moments her servant had returned with a goblet of blood. Pem drank it down ravenously.

"Does your Majesty require more?" asked her maid.

"No, but bring me my son. My breasts are swollen, I want to breastfeed him.

"Your Majesty, I don't think..."

"Now, my lady!" snapped Pem. This was complete nonsense, she was the baby's mother, he needed **her** milk.

The wet nurse entered the room with a little curtsy. She had the baby cradled in her arms and he was tightly swaddled in a blanket. Pem smiled and the woman brought him to her. Pem took the tiny baby gently in her arms.

She was almost brought to tears when she saw him, he was beautiful, with tiny ringlets of blonde hair. His eyes were open and he was looking up at her with big blue eyes. Pem was dying to rid herself of the uncomfortable feeling of

fullness in her breasts. She would nurse her own damn baby!

She lifted her right breast out of her nightgown and nudged the nipple toward the tiny baby's cheek. He turned his head eagerly toward the nipple and bit into her greedily. Pem squealed as his teeth pieced her nipple and he began to suck greedily. Pem groaned in agony as he sucked all he could from one breast, then cried angrily until she put him on the other. Pem flinched in pain and he latched on to the left breast and drained that one as well.

The wet nurse gave her a smug smile when the baby had finished and Pem handed him back. She touched one of Pem's badly disfigured nipples in pity.

"I'll get you some cream for those. I tried to tell you, your Majesty. Not all nipples are cut out for that kind of abuse. Mine are all hardened up, I got years of experience," said the woman, proudly.

Pem nodded sheepishly, perhaps this woman was right and she was not cut out to nurse a vampire baby. The uncomfortable fullness in her breasts was now gone, but her nipples were sore and abused. She decided that a wet nurse was a good thing. Something she would appreciate fully, once her own breast milk had dried up.

Pem rested all day, at sunset Salinar arrived to check on her before he left for court.

"Good evening your Majesty, how are you feeling?"

"I am feeling well my Lord, though still a bit tired," breathed Pem.

"You will stay here and rest tonight. You will not be expected in court for a few days. On Saturday we will present our baby to the Kingdom."

Pem smiled, she was glad she didn't have to go to court tonight, she barely had the strength to get out of bed.

"We still need to decide on a name for our son," said Salinar, smiling at her.

"I shall think about it tonight, while you are at court."

Salinar came and sat on the side of the bed and placed his hand on her cheek, gently sweeping her hair off her face.

"I thank you my Lady, for giving me such a beautiful son. I am forever grateful," he said, smiling into her eyes.

Pem placed his hand in both of hers and kissed it. She almost felt bad for cheating on him with his brother, but not quite. She loved Persius, she knew it in her heart. The only problem was, what to do about it? Truly, there was nothing she could do about it, she was forever enslaved to be married to Salinar.

"He is quite beautiful, I think he takes after his dad."

"That is where you are wrong, your Majesty. He is beautiful like his mother."

Salinar kissed her deeply. Pem was happy enough to kiss him back. There was no use dreaming about a man she could never have, her future was with Salinar, she would do her best to be happy about it.

The kiss deepened and Salinar, slid his hand into the bodice of her dress and cupped her breast, giving her nipple a pinch. Pem jumped and cried out.

"Good Lord, what the hell?" exclaimed Salinar, Pem's shout had frightened him.

Pem lifted her breast from her bodice and showed him her bloody and bruised nipple. Salinar gawked at it in shock.

"What in God's name has happened to you!" he exclaimed.

"I decided I wanted to breastfeed the baby," said Pem, giving him a wry smile.

"I hired a damn wet nurse, where the hell was she?" he boomed.

"She tried to warn me, but I wanted to..."

"Darling have you forgotten, we're vampires..."

"Yes, I know. I won't forget that again," said Pem rolling her eyes miserably.

Salinar went on to court and left his wife in bed to recover and get some much needed rest. It was a festive night in the great hall, everyone was excited about the birth of the new Prince, though Salinar still hadn't given out many details. He hoped to wait till the official presentation on Saturday, when they'd decided on a name.

Later that evening Salinar spotted his brother alone glancing out the window.

"What is the matter brother?" asked Salinar.

"Nothing, just enjoying a moment of solitude. You forget, I am not used to the rigorous social duties of court," said Persius, with a bit of a frown

"You should be enjoying being the most eligible bachelor in court. I have never seen so many woman flocked around one man," said Salinar.

"As if I could chose one," said Persius.

"At least you are not the family heir, you may choose if you wish. My marriage was arranged, I was betrothed to my wife, neither of us had any choice in the matter."

"But Pem is magnificent, how could you possibly want someone else?"

"She is beautiful and intelligent, but personally, I would have preferred a woman a bit more demure and obedient. That woman is frightfully headstrong, you have no idea," said Salinar, shaking his head miserably.

"That is the part that makes her so magnificent."

"That is the part that makes me so worried. The woman has a mind of her own. If she were to get it into her brain to defy me, think of the trouble I would have."

"I see your point, how is she feeling?" asked Persius. He was dying to stop by and see her for himself, but of course, that would be frowned upon.

"I want to say she is doing well, but the little fool had a bit of a mishap today."

"What sort of mishap?" asked Persius.

"Do not worry, she will be fine once her nipples heal up. She thought she would send the wet nurse away and breastfeed the baby herself."

"Oh my, didn't anyone warn her?'

"I believe they tried, but she wouldn't listen," said Salinar, giving his brother a sly smile.

"Poor baby, of course she didn't grow up in our culture, she has a lot to learn. I'm sure she didn't realize the little monster would be born with teeth."

"Well she realizes it now." said Salinar with a laugh.

CHAPTER TWENTY THREE

On Saturday Pem and Salinar prepared for the formal presentation of their son, the Prince. The seamstress had made a special outfit for the baby as well as Pem and Salinar.

He would be presented Claudius Lucentio of Milan, the Duke of Barrington, second in line to the throne after Alexander, who was also had a new outfit for the occasion. He was growing so quickly now, nothing seemed to fit him for long. He was now the size of a four year old child and so smart he could read and write in English, French, Italian and Latin. Pem had no doubt he would be an excellent King someday.

The formal ceremony was beautiful and the entire kingdom was seemed to be quite pleased with their new Prince. Salinar was just pleased that the Milan family was back in power. If he had anything to do with it, Pem feared she would be pregnant immediately, Salinar wanted lots of heirs, just in case.

Having a male child was good, as that ensured the current bloodline would stay in power, though female heirs were also coveted, as they could be used as bargaining chips. Many a coven feud was put to rest by marrying off of daughter to the son of a rival coven.

Pem had Claudius cradled in her arms as they stepped back in from the balcony where they had addressed their kingdom. Alexander walked behind her clinging to her skirt. Salinar was jubilant, his face was beaming with excitement.

The room was filled with family. Ludmilla stepped forward to hug her daughter and get her first glance of the new Prince.

"He's adorable darling. I am so proud of you," said her mother.

"Thank you mother," said Pem.

Pem made her way around the room to visit with the others who wanted to congratulate her. She finally arrived in front of Persius. It was hard to remain distant, she wanted to throw her arms around him, she had missed him this past week.

"Congratulations, he's beautiful," he said, giving her a sincere smile.

Pem gave him a serene smile, trying her best to appear aloof to the others in the room.

"Thank you, dear brother. I appreciate everything you've done for Salinar and I."

A bit later the reception was winding down, the nanny had taken the children for their naps and most of the visitors had left. Pem's mother approached her once more to say her good byes.

"I guess I'll be on my way. it was good seeing all of you. I just have one question for you, though it may seem a bit personal."

"What's that mother?" asked Pem, resisting the urge to roll her eyes.

"What is your relationship with Salinar's brother, Persius?"

"I don't know, he's like a brother in law, I guess. Why do you ask?"

"I'm just worried about you darling."

"Why would you possibly be worried about me?"

"Because you are notoriously headstrong and I couldn't help but notice the poor fool couldn't take his eyes off of you for even a moment. When you spoke to him, you blushed."

"There is nothing to worry about mother," snapped Pem, looking around nervously.

"Pem darling, please realize that though our culture as a whole doesn't frown upon adultery, the royal family is the one exception. As King consort Salinar is your Lord and Master and the legitimacy of his offspring must be guaranteed. An affair in the royal family would not be tolerated by the coven."

"I realize that mother, you are worried about nothing."

"I seriously doubt that, but remember who you are and what your position means. No sexual encounter is worth being burned to death."

Pem shivered, thinking for a brief moment, about Fortuno and how he had died a horrible death. Alexander's angelic face was now all she had to remind her of her husband who lost his life over a foolish tryst.

"I am married to Salinar, he is the father of Claudius. I will not ruin my marriage."

"I hope not," snapped her mother with a bit of a scowl.

Pem frowned as she watched her mother leaving. She hoped it wasn't quite that obvious for everyone. She was in love with Persius, but she was no longer pregnant, it was no longer safe for them to be together. If she were to end up pregnant with Persius' child, they would both be burned for treason.

Many weeks passed, Pem intentionally kept herself busy with the children. She didn't need to, as Queen, they had nannies to care for them. She loved spending time with them and they were growing so fast, they wouldn't be babies for long. She saw Persius occasionally at court, but only in passing, he too seemed eager to keep a bit of distance between them, it would be dangerous if anyone suspected that they had been lovers.

Salinar had been hinting that he was ready for Pem to be pregnant again. He wanted a daughter, a beautiful little girl to betroth to the Count of Palermo's son, Matteo.

Pem wasn't ready to be pregnant again, but she knew if she put him off too long it was likely that Salinar would look to courtesans to fulfill his sexual needs. That was something that absolutely made her blood boil. She was expected to be faithful to her husband, but her husband could basically do however he saw fit. It was maddening!

That evening, Pem was reading in bed and there was a knock at the door. She assumed it was her maid.

"Come in," she called.

Her face almost fell when she realized it was Salinar. It would be hard to put him off, now that he had arrived in her bed chambers. Obviously, he was very serious about having another child.

"Hello darling," he said, smiling at her.

"Hello my Lord, have you come to kiss me good night?" she asked, hopefully.

"That among other things," he told her with a sly smile as he unfastened the top button of his collar.

"Salinar, I wish you would give me a few more weeks. Childbirth is so exhausting, I barely just began to feel normal again," she whined.

"My darling we are royalty, it is your duty to produce heirs. We need a daughter to pledge to the Count of Palermo, otherwise his loyalties will go to another. We desperately need that marriage contract."

Pem sighed miserably, just like she had been, her daughter would be nothing but a bargaining chip in this great game of politics.

"It hardly seems right to have her married off before she's even conceived."

"Welcome to our crazy world, I'm sure it sounds incredibly barbaric to yourself, coming from the 'civilized world' as you did." he seethed.

"It may seem less civilized to you, but at least in my world the woman are free to marry who they chose, at least most of them are."

"And does this work out well for them?"

Pem almost giggled, perhaps he was right. When more than fifty percent of all marriages were now ending in divorce, maybe one's own judgement was not a reliable factor in picking a mate.

"I'm afraid not," she giggled.

"You see, then we are doing our daughter a favor. We will have her safely ensconced in a good family with an expansive estate, a title and we'll have earned respect for our own coven in the process."

"I understand my Lord, but still, you are so anxious to bring another child into the world, while I absolutely detest the thought of being pregnant again. The first time was bad, this past pregnancy was worse, I imagine this one will be worse still."

"I imagine that is a possibility," said Salinar, who was now unable to look her in the eye.

He realized why she didn't want to be pregnant again, but they needed a daughter and soon, lest the Count betroth his son to another.

"Please darling, what is it your peers say? Take one for the team?"

Pem sighed miserably, it seemed there was no getting the idea out of his head. Salinar had decided that they needed a daughter, and he was determined to conceive her tonight. Pem reluctantly pulled back the sheets and patted the spot next to her.

Salinar gave her a huge grin and undressed in record speed. In an instant it seemed, he was in the bed and was kissing her ardently. Pem was trying to relax, but regrettably, she wasn't feeling aroused at all.

Salinar didn't really notice her lack of enthusiasm, he trailed his hand down her flat stomach to the soft folds, which he parted gently with his fingers. He found her clitoris and began massaging it, in an effort to arouse her. He dipped a finger into her, he was stunned to find she wasn't really wet at all.

"Relax my darling, everything is going to be fine," he breathed into her ear.

"Easy for you to say, you don't have to be pregnant," sighed Pem.

"I know what I have to do to get you to give in," said Salinar, sliding his face down between her legs so that he could use his tongue to help lubricate her. He buried his face between her legs using his tongue to make her writhe and moan.

Just when Salinar thought she was ready for him to enter her, she spun around and took his cock into her mouth. He gasped in pleasure as she let the whole thing slide slowly into her mouth and throat. He had only intended to let her suck it for a few moments. He knew exactly what she was trying to do, divert him from his goal. He almost laughed out loud, it would not be that easy to divert his attention.

Unfortunately, he had underestimated her talents, It felt so good it only took him a few moments before he blew his load. Soon he had fallen asleep and was snoring softly. Pem smiled to herself, even though she knew he would be back tomorrow night.

When the sun rose Salinar got up and went to his own chambers. He preferred his own room, it was darker, as the light really bothered his eyes. Pem usually didn't mind her east facing room too much, she usually slept through the brightest part of the day, she usually woke up early so that she could go to the sitting room and watch the sun set.

Shortly after Salinar left, there was a knock at the door. She called to the knocker to enter, since it was probably Salinar.

Pem was startled to see Persius standing there. She pulled the satin sheets up over her body, she was only wearing a thin gauze nightgown.

"I'm sorry to disturb you. I just..."

"You just what?" asked Pem.

"I missed you. I love you. I know we can never be together, but I had to see you."

Pem wanted to run into his arms, but she couldn't. She had missed him too. If she touched him now, she might not be able to stop. She wasn't pregnant, she couldn't risk being with him and conceiving a bastard child, they'd both be burned.

"Persius, you shouldn't be here."

"I know that. It's just that..." he sighed, he wasn't sure what he wanted to say.

"Persius, I want you. I love you, but we can never be together. I think you know that."

Persius nodded and took a step toward the door.

"Wait!" cried Pem, running into his arms.

Persius gathered her into his arms and kissed her and she kissed him back with a passion she didn't even know existed in her. In moments they were both gasping breathlessly.

Persius trailed kisses down her neck to her right breast, then he took her nipple into his mouth and sucked it hard as Pem gasped in pleasure. He picked her up and carried her to the bed.

"Why aren't you pregnant yet?" he asked smiling into her eyes.

"I won't let Salinar make love to me, I can't bare the thought of being pregnant again," said Pem.

"Did you know you are positively luscious when you are pregnant? Besides, once you are pregnant I can do whatever I want and not worry."

"I know, it's just that..."

Pem couldn't say another word, Persius had worked his way down her body and was now between her legs flicking his tongue into her in such a way she thought her entire body would turn inside out in an attempt to bring his tongue into her deeper. In a matter of moments she was shuddering with an orgasm, but he didn't stop, he kept working his tongue and lapping up her juices like a cat lapping up warm milk.

Pem was shuddering and writhing around on the bed like a madwoman. She could barely catch her breath. Then in a matter of seconds he was kneeling over her, Pem wanted to tell him no, but she couldn't. She shuddered as he dipped his cock into her, but then he took it out. Pem was glaring at him as if he were crazy, but he flashed her a sly smile. He flipped her over and pulled her up by her hips until she was on all fours and he slowly began to push his cock into her tight little ass.

It took a few moments but soon he had the whole thing in her ass and he was moving inside her slowly. Pem was almost ready to cum, but it felt so good, she didn't want it to end. Persius was close as well so it seemed as if there was no putting it off, he rammed into her one more time and Pem dissolved into spasms of an all consuming orgasm, Persius followed suit by filling her with his own dramatic orgasm. They both collapsed on the bed giggling.

Persius gathered her into his arms and held her till they both fell asleep. Pem woke up just before sunset. She shook Persius awake, worried that Salinar would show up soon.

He dressed quickly and kissed her before he disappeared into the shadows of the corridor. He had but one thing to ask her before he left.

"Let Salinar get you pregnant tonight, then we can do as we wish."

Pem frowned as he left, if only it were that easy. It would still be cheating, she already felt incredibly guilty. She was the Queen for God's sake, what was she doing? Screwing around with the King's brother, was he really worth losing everything over?

That night at court Pem was happy to be joining the dancing and other festivities, she missed doing all these things when she was pregnant. Not long before dawn Salinar claimed his wife from the dance floor and led her to the stairway. Ludmilla gave her an encouraging smile. It was obvious to everyone, Salinar was desperate to have another heir and he was determined to conceive her tonight.

He took Pem by the hand and led her up the stairs to her chambers. When they were inside he turned to her and gave her a sardonic smile.

"I believe you deceived me last night," he said, regarding her casually.

Pem was froze in place, her mind was turning with thoughts of her affair with Persius. Did Salinar somehow know? She was almost certain he did not, she took a deep breath to calm her nerves.

"Deceived you my Lord? I'm afraid I don't know what you are talking about."

"You used that talented little mouth of yours to satisfy me and I fell asleep without attaining my goal. Tonight though, I

will not be put off. We will conceive our daughter, do you understand, your Majesty?" his voice had a stern tone, Pem almost shuddered.

"It's not my fault darling, you know how much I love to have your amazing cock in my mouth and..."

"Not another word my love," he said, placing a finger over her lips. "You will submit to your Lord and Master, will you not?"

"Yes my Lord," said Pem, her voice resigned.

"Do not sigh as if you are being punished. This is your duty, my Queen. Besides, I have a slight suspicion that you are dying to get your hands on my brother, perhaps this pregnancy will give you another such opportunity. Another threesome perhaps?"

"I did enjoy the threesome" said Pem, flashing him a sly smile.

"Yes, I'm trying my best to forget just how much you enjoyed it," he told her grimly.

"If we put off my getting pregnant, you could have me all to yourself," said Pem, her voice was teasing.

"I"ll take my chances," said Salinar.

"Yes, my Lord," said Pem, giving him a slight curtsy.

Salinar smiled and led Pem to the bed, he undressed her slowly, his eyes roaming over her body was a feast for his senses. Pem began to undress him as well, she gave him a seductive smile as she reached for his cock but he pushed her hand away."

"No darling, if you think a blow job is going to satisfy me tonight, you're wasting your time. There will be no foreplay this time, you will spread your legs and give me the child I desire," he snapped. Pem almost cringed at his harsh tone.

Unwilling to waste anymore time, he pushed her onto her back roughly and shoved his cock into her, ready or not. Pem gasped in surprise, as he buried the entire length of his cock inside her. She shuddered uncomfortably, he was usually a bit more gentle with her. His cock was so thick, he was usually careful not to try and jam the entire thing into her with his first stroke, but obviously tonight he could care less.

Pem almost shuddered when she saw the look on this face, it was so determined. Of course, they'd had rough sex before but this was soulless, almost malicious. Salinar was ramming into her again and again, his face a mask of blind fury. He was determined that Pem get pregnant tonight, no matter what the consequences.

As tenacious as he was, he had obviously forgotten that in order to conceive, his wife must climax as well. Regrettably the experience wasn't all that sensual for Pem. She felt like an object and she just lay there wishing he would finish until finally, he came inside her. He was gasping and shuddering, he had absolutely no idea that Pem hadn't climaxed as well.

After he finished, he pulled her into his arms and kissed her, in moments he had fallen asleep. Pem was laying there staring at the ceiling, so angry she could barely see straight. He had basically fucked her like she was nothing but a prostitute. He could have cared less about her pleasure.

Pem shook her head miserably and rested her hand on her stomach as she stewed over her husband's self centered love making skills. In moments her anger had passed and she was suddenly feeling very smug, Salinar still hadn't accomplished his goal. Her abdomen was cool, her womb

was empty, there was no baby burning inside of her, they hadn't conceived.

She almost giggled, she was like a practiced courtesan. She had no orgasm, so she had not gotten pregnant from this encounter. She was so happy she felt like laughing out loud and teasing him, but he was snoring softly, it was best not to wake him.

CHAPTER TWENTY FOUR

Pem was awakened by a harsh band of light filtering into her room. The sunlight seeping through the gap in the drapes was blinding, she opened her eyes for just a second but it was almost painful, she squeezed them shut again. She pulled the satin sheets up over her face, she was too tired to get up and adjust the drapes.

She was startled to feel a bit of movement in the bed next to her. Apparently, Salinar was still there in bed with her, despite the fact that he usually vacated her room before sunrise. His room was on the west side of the castle, protected from the morning sun.

Before she knew it, Salinar was kissing her cheeks, kissing her neck, trailing kisses down her abdomen. She was still so tired, she couldn't open her eyes, but it felt so good, there was no use pushing him away, even though she was still a tiny bit angry with him.

The kisses were trailing lower still and soon Pem had a small smile on her face as he was pushing her legs apart and burying his face between them.

Pem was happy that he was trying to make up for being such a self centered lover last night. She moaned at the exquisite feel of his soft, wet tongue licking her, enticing her. She wanted to peek a bit, just to see the expression on his face but she was still so tired, her eyelids refused to budge.

"Are you trying to apologize for being such an ass last night?" she teased.

Salinar did not answer, but soon his tongue began working faster, causing her hips to buck and her head to roll uselessly on the pillow. His tongue kept prodding, licking

and slurping greedily until she was taken over the edge with a glorious climax.

Pem could barely catch her breath, she was laying there panting, still unable to open her eyes. If Salinar wanted to tell her he was sorry, he was doing a damn good job.

She knew he wasn't finished with her yet, he wanted a daughter and she knew exactly what was coming, though at this point she was feeling so good, she would give him whatever he wanted. She could feel Salinar moving over her body, he was looming over her and though her eyes were still closed, she knew he was ready to enter her. She was ready as well, her entire body was trembling with desire.

Finally, she felt him settle on top of her, slowly guiding his cock into her hot, wet pussy. Pem sighed as he finally slid inside her, but her ecstasy was short lived. Something was not right. She knew exactly what her husband felt like when they made love. Salinar was so large, it was almost uncomfortable for her when he first slid inside her.

This was different somehow, this cock was large, but not so thick to be uncomfortable. This was not her husband...

Pem forced her eyes open quickly, suddenly afraid that some marauder had snuck into her room. It was not a scary stranger who crept into her room, but Persius. He was smiling into her eyes as his hips set the rhythm for the thrusts that threatened to take her over the edge. Pem was panicking, this couldn't be happening.

"Persius, no," she cried, trying in vain to push her husband's brother off of her.

"It's okay my darling, Salinar told me he got you pregnant last night."

"No Persius, no!" cried Pem, trying to keep him from thrusting somehow. She was so close to an orgasm, her entire body was shaking in anticipation.

"It's okay my love. Just say yes you want it," said Persius, slamming into her even harder, his hips now moving even faster. Pem was trying to physically push him off of her, but it was impossible. She was panicking, she was so close to orgasm, he needed to pull out now, before he got her pregnant!

"Please Persius, you must stop, I'm not..." Pem couldn't finish. Her words dissolved into a mournful moan as her entire body convulsed with an intense orgasm. Persius came inside her seconds later with a loud groan. Pem was nearly brought to tears as she felt him spasm inside her, her body continued to spasm as well, thus drawing his semen into her womb. It was done, she was ruined.

When he had finally recovered a bit, Persius gathered Pem into his arms and realized that she was crying hysterically.

"My darling, what is wrong? I wanted to surprise you, I have missed you so much. I thought that you loved me."

"I do love you Persius but I didn't realize it was you. I thought that you were Salinar."

"I would have thought that my lovemaking skills were much better than Salinar's."

"I'm dead serious Persius, we are in so much trouble."

"Why do you say this my love?"

"Oh my God, how do I say this?"

"What?"

"When he made love to me last night we were both angry."

"I don't understand."

"It was all about him. I didn't come. I wasn't pregnant...till now."

Persius gasped as he suddenly realized what had happened. He had come to Pem to surprise her after his brother had told him she was with child. He had thought it would be safe. Salinar didn't realize that his wife didn't have an orgasm, the key to conceiving a child.

Pem was still crying hysterically, Persius didn't know what to do. This was a nightmare, if the courts found out that they had conceived an illegitimate child they would both be burned. Suddenly, he had an idea.

"Shhhh, darling, please calm down. Perhaps you are not pregnant."

"I am...feel," said Pem, taking his hand and placing it on her abdomen which was now burning hot.

Persius grimaced, what were they going to do? Their only hope would be to convince Salinar that the child was his. He had just told him that he'd gotten her pregnant, he had no clue that she wasn't. His arrogant brag was the only reason Persius had come to Pem's room in the first place. It was stupid, Persius had simply assumed she was pregnant again, he had been blinded by his desire to continue their affair.

"Pem darling, listen to me. We have to convince Salinar that this child is his. He has no reason to believe otherwise, okay?"

"But he will soon know..."

"No he won't, you'll have the baby, no matter what, the child is a Milan."

Pem was still crying.

"You have to straighten up, you have to convince Salinar that this baby is his, do you understand."

"I don't think I can do that," cried Pem. Her entire body was shaking and she couldn't stop crying.

"Why the hell not?" cried Persius, she was totally freaking out and it was getting on his last nerve.

"The baby is a boy," said Pem, her sobbing was now taking over her entire body. There was no getting out of this. They were both doomed to die.

CHAPTER TWENTY FIVE

Pem was determined to ride out this scam as long as she possibly could but she had no hope for the future. How could she? She wondered how she could possibly be pregnant with another boy. Perhaps she was wrong, but her brain had been telling her since the moment of conception that her child was a boy.

She hadn't said a word to Salinar, who was happy as could be about the prospect of a daughter. A daughter he could marry off to the Count of Palermo's son, Matteo. It would bond their coven to the Count's thus averting tensions and possible wars between the two covens. Hopefully Salinar hadn't promised, but Pem was almost certain that he had.

It had been two weeks since her tryst with Persius, they had been trying to come up with a plan, but what could they do? This baby was supposed be a girl, something was very tragically wrong.

That evening at court Pem was distressed to see that her mother had showed up. Her mother had unusual powers and a strong intuition. She would know in an instant that Pem was carrying a bastard child.

Pem was wearing a dark blue velvet dress with a fitted bodice that made her waist look tiny. She hadn't started to show yet, but she knew she would in a matter of days, then Salinar would insist on announcing her pregnancy.

Pem nearly cringed when she saw her mother approaching her excitedly. She sighed miserably, it was too late to run away and hide.

"Hello darling," said her mother, giving her a half hearted hug.

"Hello mother."

Without even asking, her mother placed her hand on her daughter's abdomen. She closed her eyes in concentration, Pem frowned.

"Well I'll be damned, you are pregnant. I was worried you were still being stubborn and putting your dear husband off," said her mother, flashing her a bit of a smug smile.

Pem sighed and rolled her eyes miserably.

"Wait a minute," said her mother, her face suddenly shocked.

"What?" sighed Pem.

"It's a boy, I know it is. How the hell can you be pregnant with a boy? You're supposed to have a daughter, she's to be betrothed to the Count of Palermo's son!" cried her mother,she was so stunned, her eyes threatened to bulge right out of their sockets.

"Shhhh!"

"What's going on Pem? How can you possibly be pregnant with a boy? It's not the way of things. A woman's second child is a girl, that's how it always is, that is how a vampire's body is designed," cried Ludmilla, she was shaking her head slowly in denial.

"Perhaps in the way of things, it is a man's second child that is a girl," breathed Pem.

"What?"

"I am sure it has nothing to do with the woman, I believe a mans' second child is a girl. I've been thinking about this, I

imagine that the reason I've never had a girl, is because I've never had two children with the same man," sighed Pem, there was absolutely no lie she could tell her mother that would justify her condition, it was best to just tell her.

Ludmilla was staring blankly at her. For a moment it seemed she was unable to comprehend the meaning of Pem's words. Then her mother gasped in disbelief, as she finally comprehended the full meaning of her daughter's fate. A look of bewilderment flashed across her face.

Pem was now worried her mother would start a fight with her and cause a scene there in the great hall, as if she had done any of this on purpose. Sadly her mother did something else Pem had not expected, Ludmilla fainted...

Nothing like a little drama to liven up a dull night at court. Pem could only feign innocence as several men hauled her mother away to her room so that she could recover. The crowd was incredulous, why would Ludmilla just faint like that?

Vampires didn't just faint and Ludmilla was one of the strongest of their kind. Pem was suddenly worried, what if her mother inadvertently told someone her secret while she was in a state of shock? When the crowd had dispersed a bit, Salinar came over to Pem and took her by the arm.

She hadn't seen him all night, but she was suddenly glad to have him here by her side right now. She was feeling a little shaky herself at the moment, her calm facade was rapidly drifting away.

"That was odd," said Salinar, waving his hand in the general direction that her mother had been carted off in.

"My mother is always a little odd," said Pem, monitoring her voice, hoping he didn't notice the quiver of anxiety, she couldn't hide.

"Truly," said Salinar, raising his glass to her in a toast.

Pem frowned, for now it was probably best that he was slightly inebriated, but he'd grown rather fond of wine lately and she didn't like it one bit. Salinar tended to be a bit of an ass when he'd been drinking and it was beginning to be a bit of a pattern.

"You look so beautiful tonight. Pregnancy makes you even more radiant than ever," said Salinar, giving her a sly smile.

"Thank you my Lord," said Pem giving him a small curtsy. She smiled back at him even though she suspected that the compliment really only meant he was drunk and horny.

"What do you say we slip away for a bit?"

"To our rooms? It's much too early, people would talk," said Pem.

"There's no need to go to our rooms," said Salinar, pulling her into an alcove and drawing the heavy velvet drapes around them. He took her into his arms and began kissing her. Pem was a bit nervous that someone might discover them there, behind the drapes, but now that she thought about it, she'd seen other people sneaking off together to one of the alcoves in the past, it's almost as if they were designed for that specific purpose.

The castle's alcoves were stone outcroppings where windows were built in to allow light in through the thick stone walls. Each alcove was about eight feet deep and nearly as wide. There was a narrow bench on either side and the drapes surrounded the alcove so that during the day when

the light streamed in, it was a sunny and private place to read, if you weren't a vampire, anyway.

Tonight the alcove was lit by a small candelabra and the moonlight that seeped in through the leaded glass window. It was just enough to cast a warm glow over the alcove for a quick tryst.

Salinar was already kissing her neck and pushing her gown off her shoulders to give himself access to her breasts which were already starting to swell as evidence of her pregnancy. He pushed her against the stone wall a bit too hard, as he'd had a bit too much too drink. Pem gasped as he caressed her breast, taking the nipple into his mouth and sucking hard. In a matter of moments his hands were lifting her skirts, exploring her, Pem was moaning for more. Salinar was drunk and horny, she was just horny.

Pem was just wondering how they were going to do it in this space when Salinar leaned her over so she could place her hands on the bench. He hiked up her many layers of skirts clumsily. She let out of shriek of delight when he entered her from behind.
She was trying her hardest to be quiet, since the location was not exactly private, but Salinar was penetrating her so deeply in this position, she couldn't help herself. Her unrestrained moans were ringing out loudly through the great hall. Her husband was only encouraged by her boisterous cacophony. He soon joined in with his own unreserved noisemaking which eventually ended in a crescendo of moans and grunts. Pem came just seconds later with her own mournful sounding wail.

Pem couldn't help giggling when she heard that the rambunctious crowd in the great hall had grown silent. They had obviously caused a bit of a disturbance.

"What are you giggling about, your Majesty?" asked Salinar, taking his wife into his arms and holding her on his lap tenderly.

"I believe we were too noisy and given ourselves away, everyone out there is suddenly silent."

"Well, I imagine we won't need to announce your pregnancy then," said Salinar, with a proud smile.

Pem gave him a fake smile. Poor Salinar, he was so proud and so excited to be expecting a daughter. What would he do when he found out the truth? That prospect was so scary, Pem didn't even want to think about it.

They pulled themselves together, then Salinar took her by the hand, pulled back the draperies and led her out of the room. The room was immediately filled with applause and various cheers from the crowd. Pem was blushing furiously but Salinar was nodding to the crowd and waving like a baseball player who had just hit a home run. Well, in essence he had...

The next evening Pem's maid was busy dressing her and getting her ready for court. There was a terse rap on the door.

"Come in," called Pem.

The door opened and her mother stepped in. She looked resplendent in an elaborate emerald silk gown that hugged every curve of her body. Her pale blonde hair was braided and arranged beneath her elegant headpiece. She looked more like a queen herself than a dowager grandmother to the Prince.

"Hello your Majesty," said her mother, dropping into a deep curtsy, for the sake of appearances, at least.

"Hello mother," said Pem, dismissing her maid with a nod of her head.

"Well are you going to willingly explain to me what is going on, or do I need to force it out of you?"

"There's no need to force anything, mother. I screwed up, I need your help, I don't know what to do," sighed Pem.

"If you truly screwed up in the manner that I am imagining, meaning you screwed someone other than your husband and are now carrying his child, I will tell you there is absolutely nothing I can do."

"But you have the most outstanding powers of anyone in this coven. Are you certain there is nothing you can do?"

"Yes, my powers are great, but the power of the coven is greater. Being royalty you will be held to a higher standard than anyone. If you were a mere maid carrying an illegitimate child, I imagine no one would care, but you my darling, are Queen consort, the legitimacy of your child cannot be in question."

"What if I had a miscarriage?"

"Darling, we are vampires, we don't have miscarriages."

"Is there any other way to end this pregnancy?" cried Pem, completely frustrated. Her mother had powers, surely there was something she could do.

"We can't just end our pregnancies. For one thing, the council would know immediately, the other thing is vampire pregnancies are strong, to try to damage the fetus would do more damage to the mother. The only way to end it would be to kill you."

Pem sighed, she had no idea what to do. She was doomed, should she fess up now and be tried for treason and burned? If she carried her baby to term, the fact that it was a boy, not a girl would give her infidelity away, then her shame would be complete. That prospect didn't sound any better.

"If I have the baby, what will happen to him?" asked Pem, secretly hoping the baby would be allowed to live, she knew he could never be a Prince, but he was an innocent child, surely they would have mercy on an innocent baby.

"I'm sorry Pem, I have nothing pleasant to tell you. You will be burned, your child will be burned and so will your lover."

"They can't burn my lover if I never tell them who it is," breathed Pem.

"You won't have to tell them my darling, they'll know."

"But how?" Pem was panicking, this was so unfair.

"LIke myself, the council members have many powers. If you wish to keep your secret a bit longer I recommend you keep your distance from them, lest they discover your deed before you are ready to disclose it."

"What do you mean disclose it?" cried Pem.

"Well you're not going to wait until you have the baby are you? Save yourself the humiliation and confess before it comes to that. Speak to your husband privately, if he has a bit of sympathy for you, perhaps he will send you away to another coven, that way your shame will not hang over your heirs who will take the throne regardless," said Ludmilla.

Pem smiled, at least she hadn't ruined things for Alexander and Claudius.

"Will Alexander be safe, or just Claudius?"

"I imagine that is up to Salinar and the council," said her mother, her face was grim.

"So that means no," snapped Pem.

"It's no secret that Salinar and Fortuno hated each other. Salinar gave Alexander legitimacy by giving him his name. Once your deeds are known I have no doubt he will officially repeal his legitimacy, leaving Alexander basically a nobody."

"But will he live?" gasped Pem. She hated to think that this one stupid thing she had done could ruin so many lives.

"That is entirely up to Salinar," said her mother, giving her a glance of pity and then heading to the door and letting herself out.

Pem could only dissolve into tears. How could one stupid thing ruin so many lives? Why did she fall in love with Persius in the first place? As horrible as her fate seemed, she thought to herself that she would do all again if faced with the decision. Her love for Persius was more than just an affair.

She wasn't sure what she should do. Should she tell Salinar now and beg for mercy? It seemed like that was the best option, but she was so frightened, she wasn't sure if she could.

Her maid returned to the room and found her sobbing.

"Your Majesty, what is wrong?"

"It is nothing. I guess my pregnancy has just made me a little emotional."

Pem forced herself to straighten up and her maid finished getting her ready for her appearance in court.

Pem managed to make it through the formalities of court, later everyone had broken off into small groups in the great hall, everyone was socializing and some were dancing, many were drinking.

Salinar was seated on the dais watching the dancers, Pem had a group of women around her all asking her questions about her pregnancy, which Salinar had announced tonight, much to Pem's dismay. A member of council approached Salinar and he beckoned to the man to have a seat next to him.

"Antonio, how are you?"

"I am well your Majesty."

"My queen is looking well tonight, is she not?" asked Salinar, gesturing across the room to where Pem was standing.

The man admired her for a moment, she did look radiant in her bright scarlet dress with it's low cut neckline and flowing skirt made of yards of fine silk. Her blonde hair was secured beneath an elaborate ruby encrusted tiara and she looked like the perfect queen. Antonio, though, had his misgivings about the queen. He had no evidence, but he had a feeling he could not shake, something was up.

"Yes, I was excited to hear the news of her pregnancy. Has her Majesty been feeling well?"

"Yes, though it's still early. When she was pregnant with Claudius I had my hands very full with her, the sexual and blood cravings got so intense, I finally had to arrange a blood

kill for her. Her feelings have intensified with each pregnancy, she fears this time will be even worse for her."

"Well, I do know one thing, your Majesty. Having a girl will be a little bit easier on her. It's the testosterone from the boys that makes the sexual cravings so intense. My wife was much more docile when she was pregnant with our girls, though by our third boy, I was hiding all phallic shaped objects and arranging blood kills at least every couple of days, she was completely out of control."

Salinar couldn't help but laugh, it sounded horrible but the cravings were intense, he guessed the poor women couldn't really help themselves.

"I'm glad to hear that this pregnancy might be a little easier for her, she was hesitant to be pregnant again in the first place. I would hate it if she thought I was responsible for so much agony."

The man laughed. He hoped his suspicions were all wrong about Pem, their coven needed this marriage to work and it needed as many heirs as Pem and Salinar could give them to ensure the Milan line would prevail.

Across the room, Pem had caught a glimpse of Persius. He was surrounded by adoring women and he seemed to be enjoying himself immensely. It made Pem extraordinarily jealous.

As the night wore on Pem was growing bored, Salinar was succumbing to the large amount of wine he had consumed and Persius was nowhere to be seen. Pem bid goodnight to the few ladies she had been socializing with and walked over to her husband.

"I'm ready to retire, are you coming with me?"

Salinar regarded her with bleary eyes. "I'm just going to have another drink."

"Good night then," said Pem, almost rolling her eyes as she headed toward the stairway. She was feeling a bit horny, but obviously her husband was going to be useless tonight. She was going to have to think of something else.

As she headed for the stairway a hand reached out from one of the alcoves and drew her in. She was pleasantly surprised to see Persius standing there in front of her.

"Hmmm, I had imagined you had left with someone else," said Pem, giving him a sly smile.

"Absolutely not! I was waiting for your husband to pass out, but I decided it was close enough right now."

Persius took her into his arms and began kissing her. Pem was nervous, but she couldn't resist his kisses. His hands were already moving down her body, exploring and caressing. Pem couldn't keep her own hands from wandering to the enormous bulge in his pants. She smiled to herself as he groaned in encouragement. He untied her bodice letting it fall away to expose her breasts, in seconds his hands and his mouth were eagerly exploring her.

Pem let out a sigh, conscious that they were in a very public place, she would definitely have to control herself tonight. If they weren't discrete, she might find herself in a lot of trouble.

In a few moments, Pem was almost too excited to worry about their less than private location. Persius had lifted her skirts and was exploring her with his fingers. Pem was biting on her lip to keep from crying out, then Persius grabbed her buttocks, lifted her entire body up and slid his cock into her, eliciting a low mournful sounding wail from

Pem. She wrapped her legs around him as they both tried to keep as quiet as possible in this tiny space.

The pace had been slow and deep at first, but Persius had now doubled the pace and Pem could feel herself on the brink. He finally came inside her, biting his lip to mute his groans. Pem buried her teeth into his shoulder as she convulsed with her own violent orgasm.

When they'd arranged themselves properly, Persius peeked out through the drapes, the crowd had died down considerably and only a few drunk appearing courtesans remained.

Pem snuck out first, seemingly avoiding anyone's notice. Persius waited a few minutes then, he too, made his escape.

Pem returned to her room just as the sun was rising. She crawled into bed in hopes that all her dreams would be of Persius.

CHAPTER TWENTY SIX

Pem awoke just as the sun was setting, she was ravenously hungry. She rang for her maid who appeared promptly carrying a tray with a goblet of blood. Pem dank it down quickly. The maid curtsied to her and left the room. With her thirst satisfied Pem began to get ready for court. As she sat there while her maid fixed her hair and fussed over her tiara, she realized she was extremely horny.

Instead of heading right to court she headed toward Salinar's chambers. She knocked. His footman came to the door.

"Her Majesty the Queen," announced the footman.

Salinar gave her a smile of surprise and beckoned her into the room. He waved the footman away and turned to her.

"To what do I owe this visit?" he asked with a smile.

Pem didn't answer, she just walked to him and began kissing him passionately. Salinar was surprised at her advances but he was all too happy to indulge her with whatever she wanted. Pem wasn't wasting any time. She pushed him back onto the bed, climbed on top of him and proceeded to ride him like a stallion.

Salinar had barely recovered his strength from that encounter when Pem crawled in front of him on all fours begging him to give it to her from behind. He was happy to oblige her once again.

The moon was high in the sky any they were still in bed. Pem, still not satisfied, was sliding her hand down Salinar's abdomen, in search of the thing that she couldn't seem to get enough of. He caught her hand before she reached it.

"Enough," he laughed. "We must at least make an appearance at court tonight."

"I can't help it,"said Pem, giving him a pout.

"They tell me that this pregnancy is supposed to be easier for you, since it's a girl. I can't imagine why you're so horny already, it's still very early in your pregnancy."

Pem bit her lip nervously. Maybe she would have to try and control herself a little bit more. Her behavior would have him completely suspicious.

"I just can't get enough of you," she told him.

"We need to call your maid, she's going to be upset that you've made a mess of your hair," said Salinar, ruffling her hair affectionately.

When her maid had fixed her hair and they had both regained their composure they arrived at court a full two hours late. After the formalities Pem joined the dancers. It seemed like a good way to burn off some of this energy that seemed to be overwhelming her. She saw Persius there, but they never met up. Her mother was there watching her carefully and several of the council members seemed to be watching her as well.

Salinar was busy socializing and getting his buzz on. As the first lights of the sunrise lit the room, Pem approached Salinar, she was hoping he would take her back to his chambers, but he was completely inebriated. His buddies dragged him to his feet and helped him to his room while Pem nodded to them and returned to her own chambers.

She dressed in her nightgown and pulled the drapes closed tight, she wasn't really tired, but there was no chance of her husband coming to her chambers this morning. She pulled

back the sheets of her bed and there was a soft rap on the door.

"Come in," she called, her heart almost skipped a beat with excitement.

The door opened and it was Persius, just as she'd hoped. She ran into his arms. He kissed her passionately and picked her up and carried her to the bed. He peeled back the gauzy white fabric of her nightgown so that he could kiss every inch of her body.

Her breasts had just begun to swell and her nipples were hard and sensitive, she moaned as he flicked his tongue over them, then his kisses trailed lower. Pem sighed in ecstasy as Persius buried his face between her legs and used his tongue and his lips to bring her to a powerful climax. Before she had time to recover he crawled up her body and slid his cock into her in one easy motion, the sensation of his long cock sliding into her caused her to climax again.

Persius had positioned himself so he was able to lift her hips and thrust himself deep inside her. Pem was unable to stop the shaking of her entire body, it felt fabulous. When Perisus finally came, his climax was so powerful, it threatened to shake the entire room, Pem let out a loud moan as he came inside her. When it was over she giggled, wondering what her ladies, who were just in the next room would think. She could only hope they were sound sleepers.

They stayed in Pem's bed all day making love three more times. Persius finally snuck out of her room just as the last rays of the sunset were reflecting off the trees outside her window.

This went on for the next several weeks. Pem was too consumed by her need for sex and blood to worry about her

fate, all her energy was consumed by getting what her body needed. There had been no more trysts at court, her mother and the council was watching her too closely for that. Pem only hoped that her ladies didn't hear her carrying on with Persius, their testimony might be used in her trial.

Salinar had grown distant, his need for alcohol had become as bad as Pem's need for blood and sex and they were both becoming consumed by their addictions.

Early one evening Antonio, head of the coven council was walking down the corridor that adjoined the Queen's chambers. He wanted to hand deliver a message from the Count of Palermo about his upcoming visit. As he rounded the corner he heard a door close, he backed into the shadows of a window well, hoping to catch a glimpse of who had come out of the Queen's chambers.

He was shocked to see the king's own brother, Persius, as he crept silently down the dimly lit corridor. Though Antonio was a bit shocked, he was still hopeful that Persius' visit to the Queen's chambers was perfectly innocent.

He approached the Queen's chambers and knocked lightly on the door. Instead of one of her servants opening the door, the Queen herself flung open the door. Embarrassingly enough she was wearing nothing but a thin filmy nightgown, so sheer that she might as well been naked as far as the councilman was concerned.

Antonio gasped when he saw her standing there in her state of undress. Pem was shocked as well. She ran to her bed and grabbed her dressing gown and pulled it around her quickly.

"I am very sorry, your Majesty," stammered Antonio, blushing furiously. He had essentially seen the Queen naked and he was completely embarrassed.

"I apologize as well your Grace. I was expecting my husband before court."

"Were you?" asked Antonio, he couldn't hide the sarcasm that was sneaking into his voice.

"Yes. So what is your business here, your Grace?" asked Pem, skillfully taking the focus off of her improper greeting. She had hoped it was Persius returning for one final lovemaking session before court. Salinar hadn't been to her chambers in weeks.

"I have brought you a message from the Count of Palermo. He is going to come here for a visit. He is anxious to meet your Majesty."

"Thank you," said Pem, taking the letter from his hand and dismissing him. She closed the door firmly and leaned against it in an effort to stop her shaking.

Pem knew Antonio was suspicious. Had he encountered Persius in the corridor? Pem could only hope that he hadn't.

Antonio was torn. By her behavior, he was almost certain that the Queen was having an affair with the King's own brother. He had seen him leave her room and it had not been innocent, had her servants been in the room and she been fully dressed he would have not thought anything of it, but that was not the case. Should he go to the King now, or should he investigate further first?

Antonio decided he would do a bit more research, he had other suspicions about the Queen, including the suspicion that she was not carrying the King's daughter, but the daughter of his brother. He would get all his ducks in a row before he approached the King, that way they could proceed right to her punishment.

That night at court Antonio kept a watchful eye on the Queen. She danced and socialized with all the ladies, but when Persius entered the room, she barely gave him a second glance. He did notice that Ludmilla was keeping a close eye on her daughter as well. He smiled to himself, Ludmilla had powerful insight, he guessed to ability to read her own daughter would be even stronger. Ludmilla was from a strong family with even stronger values, he knew she would never lie to him.

"Good evening, Madame," said Antonio, greeting Ludmilla with a curt bow.

"Good evening, Antonio," said Ludmilla, giving him a hug and kissing both his cheeks familiarly.

"It's good to see you back in court."

"Thank you, Antonio," said Ludmilla, who was already having misgivings about this old friend who had suddenly approached her for the first time since she made her appearance back in their kingdom.

"May I ask you a few questions about your daughter?"

Ludmilla sighed, she knew it was only a matter of time before members of the council had their suspicions about Pem's pregnancy. Unfortunately, she couldn't lie, whatever he asked, she knew she must answer truthfully. With any luck his questions would be vague and she could manage to evade him.

"What is it that you wish to know, your Grace?"

"Ludmilla, we have known each other for many years so I know you have powers and intuition. What have your

powers told you about the your daughter, the Queen's pregnancy?"

"I do know that she is pregnant. I was happy about that, knowing that she was not anxious to be pregnant again, her last pregnancy was so taxing for her."

"Is his Majesty the King, the father of this child?"

"That, I cannot tell."

"Are you being truthful with me, or are you simply trying to save the skin of your beloved daughter?"

"Your Grace, though I do possess many powers that are out of the ordinary, there are certain things that even I cannot see or predict."

"I feel you're being a bit evasive with me Madame."

"Your Grace, I cannot tell you what I do not know. If you have suspicions about the legitimacy of the King's child I imagine you must investigate, but you must realize, my powers do have their limits," said Ludmilla, flashing him an innocent smile.

Antonio gave her a curt bow and went on his way. He was certain that Ludmilla knew something, but he wasn't quite sure how to pry it out of her. He thought about questioning Persius, but if he was having an affair with the Queen, Antonio didn't want him to know they were onto him, it would be best to catch him in the act.

Pem was on the dance floor engaged in a group dance. She really didn't feel like dancing, but she needed to get to Persius without it being completely obvious to everyone. She was certain the Antonio was suspicious of them, she couldn't risk Persius coming to her room any more.

In the dance the ladies were to weave in and out the line of men, she would have just a moment to get her point across to Persius as she made her pass by him.

Pem was dancing and weaving in and out the line of men, smiling and nodding to them as she passed, when she passed Persius, she whispered to him desperately.

"We've been found out, do not come tonight," she whispered.

Persius gave her a puzzled look but nodded graciously. Pem continued down the line as nonchalantly as possible. When the dance was over Pem felt her mother sidle up behind her.

"You must stop seeing Persius. The council is on to you," said her mother, taking care to barely move her lips.

"Who says I'm seeing Persius?" teased Pem.

"No one has to say it, it's perfectly obvious. Do you not realize, your life is on the line?"

"I'm as good as dead mother, admit it. I'm simply buying my time till I have to deal with it. I'd have dealt with it already but it's hard to fess up to a husband who has suddenly become a raging alcoholic."

"I imagine it is stressful, having a wife who is so completely out of control."

"In case you forgot, I was basically forced to marry him, not to mention the fact that I was demanded to bear him children."

"In case you forgot, he was the once forced to marry a disgraced slut with a bastard son he was kind enough to legitimize," seethed Ludmilla.

"He is is the King and therefore he may have sex with whatever courtesan interests him, while because I am a woman, I must be faithful to him forever."

"But alas, you haven't been."

"It was a mistake, Salinar told him that I was pregnant."

"Mistake? I'd call it a tragedy you can never recover from."

"Yes, I imagine I will pay for it with my life."

"And so your sister is the one who will take the crown after your execution."

"What?"

"What did you think would happen after your execution? Life must go on in this kingdom. The King will need to remarry. If he wants more heirs with the Venezia bloodline, I suspect that Cora will be his choice," said her mother, giving her a smug smile.

"But Cora is just a baby," cried Pem.

"He will wait for her just as he waited for you. What is a few years to wait when you have eternal life? Besides he shall have his pick of the sluts to keep him busy till Cora comes of age."

"I believe he's tired of the sluts," said Pem.

"Well I believe he's tired of you. When was the last time he actually came to your chambers?"

Pem sighed, her mother had a point, though she hadn't really minded, it only meant she could spend more time with Persius, though now the council was watching her she wondered what she would do. Her sexual cravings were growing stronger every day.

She decided if any of her urges were going to be satisfied, she better get to Salinar before he got too drunk to perform. She looked around to see where he was. He was sitting on the dais, watching the dancing, he didn't appear to have been drinking, but it was his habit, surely he had. Pem approached him and curtsied deeply.

"My Lord."

"Hello darling, have you come to sit with me?"

Pem gave him a smile and placed herself strategically on his lap, hoping to encourage him to come back to her chambers. She was horny and it was the only chance she had for satisfaction tonight.

"Are you ready to go upstairs?" she asked, flashing him a seductive smile.

"My poor dear, I've forgotten how your appetite increases when you are pregnant. I am not ready to retire for the evening, but I will take care of you in one of the alcoves," said Salinar.

"I want you to come to my chambers," said Pem, she needed more than a quickie, she wanted him to stay the night.

Unfortunately, it seemed a quickie was all she would get, for some reason Salinar was not willing to accompany her to her chambers. They had a quick tryst, but for Pem it was not

enough. She returned to her chambers alone, more frustrated than ever.

She was sitting in a chair by the fire as her maid brushed out her long blonde hair. She'd drank her fill of blood but still her body had an overwhelming need for sex. Salinar wasn't coming and neither was Persius, it seemed her frustration would be complete.

"What is the matter?" asked her maid Cordelia, who always seemed to sense her frustration.

Pem rubbed her hand over the swell of her belly, the baby was hot as a furnace inside of her and it seemed nothing could quench the fire.

"I hate being pregnant, I don't like the feelings of never being completely satisfied. The thirst, the desire, I can hardly stand it. I need sex almost constantly and lately it seems my husband wants nothing to do with me."

"He has taken a fancy to Lady Eleanor," said Cordelia.

"Lady Eleanor?"

"Yes, the wife of Sir Bertram of Pelo. I imagine it's not his fault, she is said to possess certain powers of seduction."

"That bastard, no wonder he hasn't been to my chambers in weeks!" cried Pem.

"But have you not yourself been quite taken with his brother?"

"You know about that?" cried Pem.

"My Lady, how can I not? I am not deaf," said Cordelia, laughing.

Pem laughed as well. "Well that's ended too, the council has become suspicious, he cannot come here anymore."

"What shall you do?"

"I don't know," sighed Pem.

"If your Majesty does not mind, the other ladies and I might offer you a bit of relief," said Cordelia, flashing her a sly smile.

"I guess I might as well..."

Salinar had planned on spending the night in bed with Lady Eleanor, but unfortunately, he only found her amusing when he was drunk and he had abruptly quit drinking last night. He loved the wine, but he hated the hangover, besides people were starting to talk, and it was the idle talk that had him reconsidering everything he held dear in his life.

He'd been drinking heavily last night, as had been his habit of late. He found it welcome abandon from the stresses of his duties and his life which no longer seemed to be his own.

He had laid his head down for just a moment at the table, it had been spinning so badly. Members of the court had assumed he had passed out. He was quite surprised to find in a matter of moments the rumors began to fly, and since he wasn't really passed out, he actually heard them all.

It was a horrible feeling to hear things you weren't meant to hear, but also quite enlightening. There were rumors that he was a drunk, so stressed out he was no longer capable of ruling the coven or pleasing his vivacious wife for that matter. It was rumored that his own brother was now doing that. There was also the cruel rumor that his wife was carrying his brother's child, which was absolutely unacceptable. He

decided then and there he had to get his shit together and he was going to do it tonight.

He felt bad that he had put off Pem that way, but his head was full of thoughts he just couldn't shake and he was dying to see if she really would seek solace in his brother's arms. It was a cruel trick, but as he saw it, absolutely necessary.

He waited an hour, the he headed up the stairs, when he arrived outside her bedchamber he was dismayed, but not really surprised to hear Pem's moans of ecstasy coming from her chamber. Obviously the rumors were much more than just rumors. He listened for a few moments until he was unable to stand it anymore, he was completely enraged. He burst through the door ready to confront his brother and was shocked to see Pem in bed with three of her ladies.

The four of them were naked and the three ladies were all over Pem, their lips and tongues working feverishly all over her body. He was most stunned to see that one of the women was enthusiastically servicing his wife with, what had to be the largest banana he had ever seen.

As disturbing as the scene was, it was strangely titillating. The sight of those firm female bodies writhing together in the bed was so rousing, Salinar found himself encumbered with an instant erection.

The action had stopped and all four women were staring at him with a look of shock and guilt on their faces, though when Pem saw his growing erection, a seductive smile washed across her face.

Salinar waved the women away and began anxiously undressing. The women picked up their clothes and reluctantly left the room. Pem was still panting from her exertions, as he climbed into the bed.

"You came after all," she said.

"Obviously you came first, with a banana, to be more specific," he teased.

"Darling, I would have fucked a donkey if they'd brought me one," breathed Pem as Salinar settled on top of her.

"I'm sure that can be arranged."

Pem didn't have patience for his lame attempt at humor, she grabbed his cock and slid it into her, shivering as the base slid across her clit, causing her entire body to quiver.

"Better than a banana?" he teased.

"Shut up and fuck me," moaned Pem, grabbing his buttocks in an attempt to draw him in deeper.

Now Salinar knew what Antonio meant when he said he had to lock up any phallic shaped objects around his pregnant wife. When the need was great enough, obviously any object that would fit, be used to gain satisfaction.

They made love four times, as the sun came up Salinar pulled the satin sheets over his head. He was much too tired to go back to his own chambers, besides he had a few questions to ask his wife. Now that he'd heard the rumors, he had to have answers, even if the truth was something he didn't want to hear.

R. J. HANRAHAN

CHAPTER TWENTY SEVEN

No one said being King would be easy, but Salinar had decided that this day would go down in history as the worst day of his life.

He'd heard the casual rumors, but he hadn't really believed them. The rumors that his wife was having an affair with his own brother, that their baby was, in reality fathered by Persius. It all just seemed like vicious gossip, but now, sitting there in front of the council, his worst nightmare had materialized in real life.

His wife Pem could not deny that she was pregnant with yet another boy, fathered by a man who was not her husband. The council had found all the evidence they needed to implicate Persius. The head of the council was reading the list of charges against Pem and Persius in a clear, but monotonous voice.

Pem was seated next to her counsel, with her face buried in her hands. Persius was staring blankly into space. The room was packed with everyone of importance in the kingdom and the room was deadly silent as the charges were read.

Pem had dishonored the throne and the penalty would be her life, her unborn baby's life and the life of her lover, Persius. Alexander was shown mercy, he was no longer in direct line for the crown but demoted from Prince to Duke and was spared to live on as the crown Prince's older half brother.

Pem had begged that Salinar have mercy on her, but really, how could he? Part of being a King is having the respect of your kingdom and all your subjects. How could his countrymen respect him if he allowed his wife, who had treated him so disrespectfully, to live. It would be a sign of

weakness, they would not soon forget. He may have been a fool once, but that was his limit.   There was no way around it, his Queen must die.

When the council adjourned, Pem and Persius were taken away to separate cells to spend the night before their executions.

Salinar returned to his chambers. They seemed cold and dark. He poured himself a glass of wine and stared into the fire on the hearth. His heart was beating much too fast but his body refused to relax. Tomorrow his wife, his unborn child and his brother would all be executed, and he had ordered their trial. He took a sip of his wine knowing that no amount of alcohol would ever numb his pain.

ABOUT THE AUTHOR

R. J. Hanrahan was born in Galway, Ireland, the son of banker and his mother owned a local dance studio. His father passed away suddenly when he was just seven years old. His mother was a strong and determined woman who was not about to lose the house and lifestyle his father had worked so hard for. She took up writing slightly naughty books in an attempt to supplement the family's income. The success of her books not only saved the family home, but inspired her son to write as well.

R. J. had a dream to be a film maker so he traveled to the United States to attend USC, one of the top film making schools in the world. Unfortunately he was not able to finance the huge tuition bills and the high cost of living on the west coast with his meager student loans. R. J. went to work for CBS studios writing and helping out on a popular daytime soap. While working there he met Patricia Melling and a year later the two were married. R. J. and Patricia have been married for sixteen years and they have twin boys Callum and Carrick.

The family loves to travel and they have even visited Transylvania in an effort to enrich their knowledge of one of their greatest obsessions...vampires.

www.ingramcontent.com/pod-product-compliance
Lightning Source LLC
Chambersburg PA
CBHW071147170626
46809CB00002B/803